# EMISSARY OF EVIL

To enlist an organism, you find out what it wants, and give it a little in a way that indicates promise of more. The Medusa asked Gurlick what he wanted.

"What do I want?" whispered Gurlick. He ceased, for the moment, to use words, but the concepts were there. They were hate and smashed faces, and the taste of good liquor.

Deftly, the Medusa began making promises. The rewards described were described vividly indeed, and in detail that enchanted Gurlick.

At last, "Oh, sure, sure," Gurlick said. "I'll find out about that, about how people can get put together again. An' then, boy, I gon' step on their face."

So it was, chuckling, that Daniel Gurlick went forth to conquer the world. . . .

**Books by Theodore Sturgeon**

The Cosmic Rape
E Pluribus Unicorn
Sturgeon Is Alive and Well . . .

Published by POCKET BOOKS

# Theodore Sturgeon
# The Cosmic Rape

PUBLISHED BY POCKET BOOKS NEW YORK

To Hal Speer, who was there

A shorter version of this story appeared in *Galaxy Science Fiction* magazine under the title, "To Marry Medusa," copyright © 1958 by Galaxy Publishing Corp.

**POCKET BOOKS, a Simon & Schuster division of**
**GULF & WESTERN CORPORATION**
**1230 Avenue of the Americas, New York, N.Y. 10020**

# CHAPTER 1

"I'll bus' your face, Al," said Gurlick. "I gon' break your back. I gon' blow up your place, an' you with it, an' all your rotgut licker, who wants it? You hear me, Al?"

Al didn't hear him. Al was back of the bar in his saloon, three blocks away, probably still indignantly red, still twitching his long bald head at the empty doorway through which Gurlick had fled, still repeating what all his customers had just witnessed: Gurlick cringing in from the slick raw night, fawning at Al, stretching his stubble in a ragged brown grin, tilting his head, half-closing his sick-green, muddy-whited eyes. "Walkin' in here," Al would be reporting for the fourth time in nine minutes, "all full of good-ol'-Al this an' hiya-buddy that, an' you-know-me-Al, and how's about a little, *you*-know; an' all I says is I know you all right, Gurlick, shuck on out o' here, I wouldn't give you sand if I met you on the beach; an' him spittin' like that, right on the bar, an' runnin' out, an' stickin' his head back in an' callin' me a ——" Sanctimoniously, Al would not sully his lips with the word. And the rye-and-ginger by the door would be nodding wisely and saying, "Man shouldn't mention a feller's mother, whatever," while the long-term beer would be clasping his glass, warm as pablum and headless as Ann Boleyn, and intoning, "You was right, Al, dead right."

Gurlick, four blocks away now, glanced back over his shoulder and saw no pursuit. He slowed his scamper to a trot and then a soggy shuffle, hunching his shoulders against the blowing mist. He kept on cursing Al, and the beer, and the rye-and-ginger, announcing that he could take 'em one at a time or all together one-handed.

He could do nothing of the kind, of course. It wasn't in him. It would have been success of a sort, and it was too late in life for Gurlick, unassisted, to start anything as new and different as success. His very first breath had been ill-timed and poorly done, and from then on he had done nothing right. He begged badly and stole when it was absolutely safe, which was seldom, and he rolled drunks providing they were totally blacked out, alone, and concealed. He slept in warehouses, box-cars, parked trucks. He worked only in the most extreme circumstances, and had yet to last through the second week. "I'll cut 'em," he muttered. "Smash their face for them, I'll . . ."

He sidled into an alley and felt along the wall to a garbage can he knew about. It was a restaurant garbage can and sometimes . . . He lifted the lid, and as he did so saw something pale slide away and fall to the ground. It looked like a bun, and he snatched at it and missed. He stooped for it, and part of the misted wall beside him seemed to detach itself and become solid and hairy; it scrabbled past his legs. He gasped in terror and kicked out, a vicious, ratlike motion, a hysterical spasm.

His foot connected solidly and the creature rose in the air and fell heavily at the base of the fence, in the dim wet light from the street. It was a small white dog, three-quarters starved. It yipped twice, faintly, tried to rise and could not.

When Gurlick saw it was helpless he laughed aloud and ran to it and kicked it and stamped on it until it was dead, and with each blow his vengeance became more mighty. There went Al, and there the two bar-flies and one for the cops, and one for all judges and jailers, and a good one for everyone in the world who owned anything, and to top it, one for the rain. He was a pretty big man by the time he was finished.

Out of breath, he wheezed back to the garbage can and felt around until he found the bun. It was sodden and slippery, but it was half a hamburger which some profligate had tossed into the alley, and that was all that mattered. He wiped it on his sleeve, which made no appreciable difference to sleeve or bun, and crammed the doughy, greasy mass into his mouth.

He stepped out into the light and looked up through the mist at the square shoulders of the buildings that stood around to watch him. He was a man who had fought for, killed for what was rightfully his. "Don't mess with me," he growled at the city.

A kind of intoxication flooded him. He felt the way he did at the beginning of that dream he was always having, where he would walk down a dirt path beside a lake, feeling good, feeling strong and expectant, know-ing he was about to come to the pile of clothes on the bank. He wasn't having the dream just then, he knew; he was too cold and too wet, but he squared his shoul-

7

ders anyway. He began to walk, looking up. He told the world to look out. He said he was going to shake it up and dump it and stamp on its fat face. "You going to know Dan Gurlick passed this way," he said.

He was perfectly right this time, because it was in him now. It had been in the hamburger and before that in the horse from which most of the hamburger had been made, and before that in two birds, one after the other, which had mistaken it for a berry. Before that . . . it's hard to say. It had fallen into a field, that's all. It was patient, and quite content to wait. When the first bird ate it, it sensed it was in the wrong place, and did nothing, and the same thing with the second. When the horse's blunt club of a tongue scooped it up with a clutch of meadow-grass, it had hopes for a while. It straightened itself out after the horse's teeth flattened it, and left the digestive tract early, to shoulder its way between cells and fibers until it rested in a ganglion. There it sensed another disappointment, and high time too—once it penetrated into the neurone-chains, its nature would be irreversibly changed, and it would have been with the horse for the rest of its life. As, in fact, it was. But after the butcher's blade missed it, and the meat-grinder wrung it, pinched it, stretched it (but in no way separated any part of it from any other), it could still go on about its job when the time came. Eight months in the deepfreeze affected it not at all, nor did hot fat. It was sold from a pushcart with a bag full of other hamburgers, and wound up in the bottom of the bag. The boy who bit into this particular hamburger was the only human being who ever saw it. It looked

8

like a boiled raisin, or worse. The boy had had enough by then, anyway. He threw it into the alley.

The rain began in earnest. Gurlick's exaltation faded, his shoulders hunched, his head went down. He slogged through the wet, and soon sank to his usual level of feral misery. And there he stayed for a while.

## CHAPTER 2

This girl's name was Charlotte Dunsay and she worked in Accounting. She was open and sunny and she was a dish. She had rich brown hair with ruby lights in it, and the kind of topaz eyes that usually belong to a special kind of blonde. She had a figure that Paul Sanders, who was in Pharmaceuticals, considered a waste on an office job, and an outright deprivation when viewed in the light of the information that her husband was a Merchant Marine officer on the Australia run. It was a matter of hours after she caught the attention of the entire plant (which was a matter of minutes after she got there) that news went around of her cheerful but unshakable "Thanks, but no thanks."

Paul considered this an outright challenge, but he kept his distance and bided his time. When the watercooler reported that her husband's ship had come off second best in a bout with the Great Barrier Reef, and had limped to Hobart, Tasmania, for repairs, Paul decided that the day was upon him. He stated as much in the locker room and got good odds—11 to 2—and somebody to hold the money. It was, as a matter of fact, one of the suckers who gave him the cue for the single strategic detail which so far escaped him. He had the time (Saturday night), the place (obviously her apartment, since she wouldn't go out) and the girl. All he had to figure out was how to put himself on the scene, and when one of the suckers said, "Nobody gets into that place but a for-real husband or a sick kitten," he had the answer. This girl had cried when one of the boss's tropical fish was found belly-up one morning. She had rescued a praying mantis from an accountant who was flailing it against the window with the morning *Times*, and after she let the little green monster out, she had then rescued the accountant's opinion of himself with a comforting word and a smile that put dazzle-spots all over his work for the rest of the afternoon. Let her be sorry for you, and . . .

So on Saturday night, late enough so he would meet few people in the halls, but early enough so she wouldn't be in bed yet, Paul Sanders stopped for a moment by a mirror in the hallway of her apartment house, regarded his rather startling appearance approvingly, winked at it, and then went to her door and began rapping softly and excitedly. He heard soft hurrying footsteps behind the door and began to breathe noisily, like someone trying not to sob.

"Who is it? What's the matter?"

"Please," he moaned against the panel, "please, please, Mrs. Dunsay, help me!"

She immediately opened the door a peering inch. "Oh, thank God," he breathed and pushed hard. She sprang back with her hands on her mouth and he slid in and closed the door with his back. She was indeed ready for bed, as he had hardly dared to hope. The robe was a little on the sensible side, but what he could see of the gown was fine, just fine. He said hoarsely, "Don't let them get me. Don't let them get me!"

"Mr. *Sanders!*" Then she came closer, comforting, cheering. "No one's going to get you. You come on in and sit down until it's safe for you. Oh," she cried as he let his coat fall open, to reveal the shaggy rip and the bloodstain, "you're hurt!"

He gazed dully at the scarlet stain. Then he flung up his head and set his features in an approximation of those of the Spartan boy who denied all knowledge of a stolen fox while the fox, hidden under his toga, ate his entrails until he dropped dead. He pulled his coat straight and buttoned it and smiled and said, "Just a scratch." Then he sagged, caught the doorknob behind him, straightened up, and again smiled. It was devastating.

"Oh, oh, come and sit down," she cried. He leaned heavily on her but kept his hands decent, and she got him to the sofa. She helped him off with his coat and the shirt. It was indeed only a scratch, laboriously applied with the tips of his nail scissors, but it was real, and she didn't seem to find the amount of blood too remarkable. A couple of cc's swiped from the plasma lab goes a long way on a white sport shirt.

He lay back limp and breathing shallowly while she flew to get scissors and bandages and warm water in a bowl, and averted his face from the light until she considerately turned it out in favor of a dim end-table lamp, and then he started the routine of not telling her his story because it was too bad . . . he was not fit to be here . . . she shouldn't know about such things, he'd been such a fool . . . and so on until she insisted that he could tell her anything, anything at all if it made

12

him feel better. So he asked her to drink with him before he told her because she surely wouldn't afterward, and she didn't have anything but some sherry, and he said that was fine. He emptied a vial from his pocket into his drink and managed to switch glasses with her, and when she tasted it she frowned slightly and looked down into the glass, but by then he was talking a blue streak, a subdued, dark blue, convoluted streak that she must strain to hear and puzzle to follow. In twenty minutes he let it dwindle away to silence. She said nothing, but sat with slightly glazed eyes on her glass, which she held with both hands like a child afraid of spilling. He took it away from her and set it on the end table and took her pulse. It was slower than normal, and a good deal stronger. He looked at the glass. It wasn't empty, but she'd had enough. He moved over close to her.

"How do you feel?"

She took seconds to answer, and then said slowly, "I feel . . ." Her lips opened and closed twice, and she shook her head slightly and was silent, staring out at him from topaz eyes gone all black.

"Charlotte . . . Lottie . . . lonely little Lottie. You're lonesome. You've been so alone. You need me, li'l Lottie," he crooned, watching her carefully. When she did not move or speak, he took the sleeve of her robe in one hand and, moving steadily and slowly, tugged at it until her hand slipped inside. He untied the sash with his free hand and took her arm and drew it out of the robe. "You don't need this now," he murmured. "You are warm, so warm . . ." He dropped the robe behind her and freed her other hand. She seemed not to understand what he was doing. The gown was nylon tricot, as sheer as they come.

He drew her slowly into his arms. She raised her hands to his chest as if to push him away but there seemed to be no strength in them. Her head came forward until her cheek rested softly against his. She spoke into his ear quietly, without any particular force or expression. "I mustn't do this with you, Paul. Don't let me. Harry is the . . . there's never been anyone but him, there never must be. I'm . . . something's happened to me. Help me, Paul. Help me. If I do it with you I can't live any more; I'm going to have to die if you don't help me now." She didn't accuse him in any way. Not once.

Paul Sanders sat quite still and silent. It wasn't easy. But sometimes when you rush things they snap out of it, groggy, even sick, but nonetheless out of it, and then that's all, brother. . . . After a silent time he felt what he had been waiting for, the slow, subsiding shiver, and the sigh. He waited for it again and it came.

The blood pounded in his ears. Well, boy, if it isn't now it never will be.

# CHAPTER 3

The carcass of the old truck stood forgotten in the never-visited back edge of a junk-yard. Gurlick didn't visit it; he lived in it, more often than not. Sometimes the weather was too bitterly cold for it to serve him, and in the hottest part of the summer he stayed away from it for weeks at a time. But most of the time it served him well. It broke the wind and it kept out most of the rain; it was dirty and dark and cost-free, which three items made it pure Gurlick.

It was in this truck, two days after his encounter with the dog and the hamburger, that he was awakened from a deep sleep by . . . call it the Medusa.

He had not been having his dream of the pile of clothes by the bank of the pool, and of how he would sit by them and wait, and then of how *she* would appear out there in the water, splashing and humming and not knowing he was there. Yet. This morning there seemed not to be room in his head for the dream nor for anything else, including its usual contents. He made some grunts and a moan, and ground his stubby yellow teeth together, and rolled up to a sitting position and tried to squeeze his pressured head back into shape from the outside. It didn't seem to help. He bent double and used his knees against his temples to squeeze even harder, and that didn't help either.

The head didn't hurt exactly. And it wasn't what Gurlick occasionally called a "crazy" head. On the contrary, it seemed to contain a spacious, frigid, and meticulous balance, a thing lying like a metrical lesion on the inner surface of his mind. He felt himself capable of looking at the thing, but, for all that it was in his head, it existed in a frightening *direction*, and at first he couldn't bring himself to look that way. But then the thing began to spread and grow, and in a few rocking, groaning moments there wasn't anything in his head *but* the new illumination, this opening casement which looked out upon two galaxies and part of a third, through the eyes and minds of countless billions of individuals, cultures, hives, gaggles, prides, bevies, braces, herds, races, flocks and other kinds and quantities of sets and groupings, complexes, systems and pairings for which the language has as yet no terms; living in states liquid, solid, gaseous and a good many others with combinations and permutations among and between: swimming, flying, crawling, burrowing, pelagic, rooted, awash; and variously belegged, ciliated and bewinged; with consciousness which could be called the skulk-mind, the crash-mind, the paddle-, exaltation-, spring-, or murmuration-mind, and other minds too numerous, too difficult or too outrageous to mention. And over all, the central consciousness of the creature itself (though "central" is misleading; the hive-mind is permeative)— the Medusa, the galactic man o' war, the superconscious of the illimitable beast, of which the people of a planet were here a nerve and there an organ, where entire cultures were specialized ganglia; the creature of which

Gurlick was now a member and a part, for all he was a minor atom in a simple molecule of a primitive cell—this mighty consciousness became aware of Gurlick and he of it. He let himself regard it just long enough to know it was there, and then blanked ten elevenths of his mind away from the very idea. If you set before Gurlick a page of the writings of Immanuel Kant, he would see it; he might even be able to read a number of the words. But he wouldn't spend any time or effort over it. He would see it and discard it from his attention, and if you left it in front of him, or held it there, he would see without looking and wait for it to go away.

Now, in its seedings, the Medusa had dropped its wrinkled milt into many a fantastic fossa. And if one of those scattered spores survived at all, it survived in, and linked with, the person and the species in which it found itself. If the host-integer were a fish, then a fish it would remain, acting as a fish, thinking as a fish; and when it became a "person" (which is what biologists call the individual polyps which make up the incredible colonies we call hydromedusae), it would *not* put away fishly things. On the contrary, it was to the interest of the Medusa that it keep its manifold parts specialized in the media in which they had evolved; the fish not only remained a fish, but in many cases might become much more so. Therefore in inducting Gurlick into itself, he remained—just Gurlick. What Gurlick saw of the Medusa's environment(s) he would not look at. What the Medusa sensed was only what Gurlick could sense, and (regrettably for our pride of species) Gurlick himself. It could not, as might be supposed, snatch out every particle of Gurlick's information and experience, nor could it observe Gurlick's world in any other way than through the man's own eye and mind. Answers there might be, in that rotted repository, to the questions the Medusa asked, but they were unavailable until Gurlick himself formulated them. This had always been a slow process with him. He thought verbally, and his constructions were put together at approximately oral speed. The end effect was extraordinary; the irresistible demands came arrowing into him from immensity, crossing light-years with considerably less difficulty than it found in traversing Gurlick's thin tough layer of subjective soft-focus, of not-caring, not-understanding-nor-wanting-to-understand. But reach him they did, the mighty unison of voice with which the super-creature conveyed ideas . . . and were answered in Gurlick's own time, in his own way, and aloud in his own words.

And so it was that this scrubby, greasy, rotten-toothed near-illiterate in the filthy clothes raised his face to the dim light, and responded to the demand-for-audience of the most majestic, complex, resourceful and potent intellect in all the known universe: "Okay, *okay*. So whaddaya want?"

He was not afraid. Incredible as this might seem, it must be realized that he was now a member, a person of the creature; part of it. It no more occurred to him to fear it than a finger might fear a rib. But at the same time his essential Gurlickness was intact—or, as has been pointed out, possibly more so. So he knew that something he could not comprehend wanted to do something through him of which he was incapable, and would unquestionably berate him because it had not been done. . . .

But this was Gurlick! This kind of thing could hold

18

no fears and no surprises for Gurlick. Bosses, cops, young drunks and barkeeps had done just this to Gurlick all his life! And "Okay, *okay!* So whaddaya want?" was his invariable response not only to a simple call but also, and infuriatingly, to detailed orders. They had then to repeat their orders, or perhaps they would throw up their hands and walk away, or kick him and walk away. More often than not the demand was disposed of, whatever it was, at this point, and that was worth a kick any time.

The Medusa would not give up. Gurlick would not listen, and would not listen, and . . . had to listen, and took the easiest way out, and subsided to resentful seething—as always, as ever for him. It is doubtful that anyone else on earth could have found himself so quickly at home with the invader. In this very moment of initial contact, he was aware of the old familiar response of anyone to a first encounter with him—a disgusted astonishment, a surge of unbelief, annoyance, and dawning frustration.

"So whaddaya want?"

The Medusa told him what it wanted, incredulously, as one explaining the utter and absolute obvious, and drew a blank from Gurlick. There was a moment of disbelief, and then a forceful repetition of the demand.

And Gurlick still did not understand.

# CHAPTER 4

I am Guido, seventeen. I . . . think; nearly seventeen. There is always doubt about us who crawled out of the bones of Anzio and Cassini as infants, as . . . maggots out of the bones when the meat is gone. I never look back, never look back. Today the belly is full, tomorrow it must be filled. Yesterday's empty belly is nothing to fear, yesterday's full belly is meaningless today; so never look back, never look back . . .

And I am looking back because of Massoni, what he has done. Massoni who will never catch me, has locked me into his house, never knowing I am here. While he goes to all the places I live, all the places I hide, I come straight here to his own house because he is not so clever as I am and will never dream I am here. Perhaps I shall steal from him and perhaps I shall kill him. Massoni's house was part of a fortification in the war, so they say, concrete walls and an iron door and little slits for windows on two sides of the single room. But at the back, where the house is buried in the hill, is plywood, and a panel is loose. Behind is space to climb. Above the room is a flat ceiling; above that a slanted roof, so there is a small space that I, Guido, would think of and he, the clever (but not clever enough) Massoni could live with for years and never suspect. I come here. I find the iron door unlocked. I slip in. I find the loose panel, the climbing space, the dark high hole to hide in, the crack to look through at the room of Massoni. There is time. It is I, Guido, he is looking for and he will look in many places before he comes back tired.

And he comes, and he is tired indeed, falling onto his bed with his overcoat on. It is nearly dark and I can see him staring up and I know he is thinking, *Where is that Guido?* And I know he is also thinking (because he talks this way), *If I could understand that Guido I could be there before he breaks the legs of another beggar, smashes the stained glass of another church, sets another fire in another print shop. . . .* If Massoni says this aloud I shall laugh aloud, because Massoni does not understand Guido and never will; because what Guido does once, Guido will never do again, so that nobody knows where Guido strikes next.

He sighs, he tightens his lips in the dimness, shakes his head hard. He is thinking, *And though he must make a mistake some day, that is not good enough. If one knew, if one could understand why, one could predict, one could be there at the time—before the time, waiting for him.*

He will never understand, never predict, and never, never be there when Guido strikes. Because Massoni cannot understand anything as simple as this: that I am Guido, and I hate because I am Guido, and I break and maim and destroy because I am Guido—because that is reason enough. Massoni is afraid because Massoni is a policeman. His life is studying things as they are, and making them into what they should be. But . . .

21

he is not like other policemen. He is a detective policeman, without the bright buttons and the stick. The other policemen catch breakers of laws so they may be punished. Some catch them and punish them too. Massoni likes to say he stops the criminal before there is a crime. Massoni is indeed not like the other police. They understand, as I understand, that a crime without witnesses and without clues is not the affair of the police, and that is why they shrug and try to forget the things Guido does. Massoni does not forget. Worse, Massoni knows which are Guido's acts and which are not. When the acid was put in the compressor tank at the bus garage and caused the ruin of sixty-one tires, everyone thought it was Guido's work. Massoni knew it was not; four different people told me what he said. He said it was not the kind of ruin Guido would make. This is why I hide. I never hid before. Eleven times I am arrested and set free, for no clues, no witnesses. I walk in the daytime and I laugh. But now Massoni knows which things I do and which I do not. I do not know how he knows that, so I hide. They are all enemies, every one, but this Massoni, he is my first and greatest enemy. They all want to catch me, *after;* Massoni wants to stop me, *before*. All the rest are making me a plague, a legend, capable of anything; Massoni credits me only with what I do, and says—and says—that I did not do this, I could not do that. Massoni makes me small. Massoni follows everywhere, is behind me; he is beginning to be at my side too often; he will be ahead of me waiting soon, if I do not take care . . . by himself he will surround me. I am Guido and I do not underestimate real danger. I am Guido, who looks and talks and behaves like any other seventeen (I think) year old, who fills the belly yesterday and today, and possibly tomorrow, any way he can, like all the others . . . but who knows there is more in life than the belly; there is the hating to be done and too short a life to do it all if I live to be a hundred and ten; there is ruin to do, breaking hurting silencing most of all silencing . . . silencing their honks and scrapes and everlasting singing.

Massoni, lying on his bed in his overcoat, sighs and rolls over and sits up. From there he can reach the little kerosene stove to light it. When the flame is blue, he sighs, yawns, lifts the kettle to shake it and put it back on the fire. He gets up slowly, walks as if his shoes are too heavy, opens the cabinet, lifts out a—

*No! Oh . . . no!*

—lifts out a portable phonograph, sets it on the table, strokes it like a cat, opens it, takes out crank, fits it in, winds it up. Goes to cabinet again, takes a record, looks, another, another, finds one and brings it to the machine—

*Not now, not now, Massoni, or you will die in a slow way Guido will plan for you.*

—puts it on, puts the needle down, and again it begins, oh why, why, why is everyone in this accursed country forever making music, hearing music, walking from one music to another and humming music while they walk? Why can Massoni not make a pot of coffee without this? It is the one thing I, Guido, cannot bear . . . and I must bear it now . . . and I cannot . . . Ah, look at the fool, swinging his hand, nodding his head, he who was too tired to move not ninety seconds ago; it is as if he drew some substitute for sleep from it, and I do believe all these fools can do it, with their dancing half the night and singing the rest . . . Why, why must

23

they have music? Why must Massoni make it now, when I am trapped up here hiding and cannot stop it and *cannot stand it* . . .

Oh look, look at him now, what is he taking from under the bed . . . surely not a . . . Oh it is, it is, it's a violin, it's that horror of shingles and catgut and the hair of horses' tails, and he, and he . . .

I will not listen, I will wrap my arms around my head, I . . . He goes now, sawing at the thing, and the caterwauling starts and I can't keep him out of my head! . . .

He plays a lot of notes, this policeman. A lot of notes. He plays with the record, note for note with the swift fall of notes from the machine.

I look at last. His feet are apart, his chin couched on the ebony rest, his eyes half asleep, face quiet, left fingers running like an insect. His whole body . . . not sways . . . turns a little, turns back, turned by the music. His right hand with the bow is very . . . wide, and free. His whole body is . . . free in a way, like . . . flying . . . But this *I cannot stand!* I will—

He has stopped.

The record is finished. He turns it over, sets down the violin on the table, winds the crank, puts on the needle again. I hold my breath, I will roar, I will scream if . . . But he is looking at the kettle, he is at the cabinet, he is fetching a cookpot, a big can with a cover. Opens. Empty. He is sighing. He goes to phonograph *(stop it, stop it)*, he stops it—only to start it over again at the beginning. He takes the big can, he—

He goes out.

Locking the door.

I am alone with this shriek of music, the violin staring up at me from its two long twisted slits.

I can run away now. Can I . . . ?

He has locked the door. Iron door in concrete wall.

And he has left his overcoat. He has left the record playing. He has left the fire in the little stove, the water about to boil on it.

He will be right back then. No time for me to pick that lock and go. I must stay here hidden and hear that gabble of music and look down at that violin, and wait, oh my God, and wait.

This country has music through its blood and bones like a disease, and a man cannot draw in a breath of air that isn't a-thrum with it. You can break the legs of a singing beggar and stop his music, you can burn the printing presses and the stacks of finished paper bearing the fly-specks and chicken-tracks by which men read the music, and still it does not stop; you can throw a brick through the shining window of a shrine and the choir practicing inside will stop, but even as you slip away in the dark you hear a woman singing to a brat, and around the corner some brainless fumbler is tinkling a mandolin. . . .

Ah, God curse that screeching record! What madness could possess what gibbering lunatic to set down such a series of squeaks and stutters? I do not know. (I will not know.) Once he did it it should have killed him, that mish-mash of noises, but they are all mad, the Frenchmen, all lunatics to begin with, and can be excused for calling it a good Italian name. Massoni, Massoni, come back and quiet this bellowing box of yours or I shall surely come down in spite of all safety and good sense and smash it along with that grinning fiddle! To be caught, to be caught at last . . . it might be worth it, for a moment's peace and a breath of air undrenched by the *Rondo Capriccioso*.

I bite my tongue until I grunt from the pain.

I do not know what they call it, that music; cannot, will not know!

Someone laughs.

I open my throat, to be silent, breathing like this, breathing like running up a kilometer of steps . . . the door moves. It is Massoni. I will kill him very soon now. It may be that for one man to dry up the music in this country is like drying up the River Po with a spoon, but oh, this one drop of music, this Massoni, surely I will scoop him up and scatter him on the bank; for if I hate (and I do), and if I hate the gurgling men call music (and I do), and if I hate policemen (and before God I do that) then in all the world I hate this maestro-detective most of all, aside and apart and above all other things. Now I know I have been a child, with my breaking here, wrecking there. Guido will be *Guido* after this killing, so now—

But the door swings open and I see Massoni is not alone, and I sink down again quiet, and watch.

He is bringing a child, an eight-year-old boy with a dirty pale face and eyes shiny-black as that damned record. They both stop as the door swings shut and listen to it, both their silly mouths agape as if they each tried to make another ear of it to hear better. And now Massoni puts down the covered can and snatches up the violin; now again he makes the chatter and yammer of notes fly up at me, along with the violin on the

26

record, and the boy watches, slowly moving his hands together until they hold each other, slowly making his eyes round. Massoni's face sleeps while the one hand swoops, the other crawls, then for a moment he looks down at the boy and winks at him and smiles a little and lets the face doze off again, playing notes the way a hose throws water-drops.

Then like slipping into warmth out of the snow, like the sudden taste of new bread to the starving, a silence falls over the room and I slump, weak and wet with sweat.

The boy whispers, "Ah-h-h, Signor Massoni, ah-h-h . . ."

Massoni puts down the violin and touches it with his fingertips, as if it were the hair of a beloved instead of a twisted box with a long handle on it, says, "But Vicente, it's easy you know."

"Easy for you, Signor . . ."

Massoni laughs. He gets covered can, opens. Puts ground coffee into cookpot, pours in boiling water, sets kettle aside, puts cookpot on stove, lowers flame, stirs with long spoon, talks.

I lie limp, wet in the dark, smelling the coffee, watching them.

Massoni says, smiling, "Yes if you like, easy for me, impossible for you. But it will be easy for you, Vicente. You have two lessons now—tonight, three, and already what you do is easy for you. When you have been playing for as many years as I have, you will not play as well as I; you will play better; you will not be good, you will be great."

"No, Signor, I could never—"

Massoni laughs and sweeps away the black bubbles on his coffee with his spoon. He lifts it off the burner and turns out the flame, and sets the pot on the table to settle. Says, "I tell you, small one, I know what is good and what is great and what is hopeless. I know better than anybody. I am a policeman, glad of what I do, and not a good violinist eating out my heart wanting greatness, because I know what greatness is. Take up the violin, Vicente. Go on, take it."

The boy takes the violin from the table and sets the ebony under his cheek and chin. He is afraid of it and he is past speech, and on him the violin looks the size of a 'cello.

"There," Massoni says, "there before you play a note, it is to be seen. Your feet placed so, to balance you when your music tilts the world. Your chest full like the beginning of a great voice which will be heard all over the earth. Throat, chin, belonging to the violin and it grown to you. . . . Put up the bow, Vicente, but don't play yet. Ah . . . there is what the violinist calls the Auer arm, and you in your eighth year, your third lesson! Now put the violin down again, boy, and sit, and we will talk while I have my coffee. I have embarrassed you."

I, Guido, watch from above with the bitter black wonder of the coffee smell pressing deep in the bridge of my nose, watch the child put down the violin exquisitely, like some delicate thing sleeping lightly. He sits before Massoni, who has poured a little coffee and much milk for him in a large cup, and is ladling in sugar like an American.

Massoni drinks his black and looks through the steam

at the boy, says, "Vicente, such a gift as yours is a natural thing and you must never feel you are different because of it . . . there are those who will try to make it so; pity them if you like, but do not listen to them. A man with talent eats, sweats, and cares for his children like any other. And if talent is a natural thing, remember that water is also, and fire, and wind; therefore flood and holocaust and hurricane are as natural as talent, and can consume and destroy you. . . . You do not understand me, Vicente? Then . . . I shall tell you a story. . . .

"There was a boy who had talent such as yours, or greater . . . oh, almost certainly greater. But he had no kind mother and father like yours, Vicente, no home, no sisters and brother. He was one of the wild ones who used to roam the hills after the war like dogs. Where he was born I cannot tell you, nor how he lived at all; perhaps some of the girls cared for him when he was a small baby. He was a year and a half old when he turned up at one of the UNRRA centers, starved, ragged, filthy.

"But you know what that baby could do, at a year and a half? He could whistle. Yes, he could. He would lie in his bundle of blankets and whistle, and people would stop and come and cluster around him.

"Perhaps if this happened today he would be cared for just for this one thing. But then, all was confusion; he was put with one family where the man died, and then into an orphanage which burned: these were unhappy accidents, but purely accidents. They could not quench the thing that was in him. Before he was three he knew a thousand melodies; he could sing words he

29

did not understand, before he could speak; he could whistle the themes of any music he had once heard. He was full of music, that boy, full to bursting."

(Above, listening, I, Guido, thought, now Massoni, who is filling you with such fairy-tales as this?)

Massoni puts his hands around the big cup as if to warm them, searches down into the black liquid as if to find more of his story, says, "Now a natural thing like talent, like pure cool mountain water, if you put it in a closed place, cover it tight, set a fire under it, nothing happens, and nothing happens, and nothing ... until *blam!* it breaks the prison and comes out. But what comes out is no longer pure cool kind water, but a blistering devil ready to scald, soak, smash whatever is near enough. You have changed it, you see, by what you have done to it.

"So. There is this small boy, three or four years old, with more music than blood in his body. And then something happens. He is taken into the family of a Corfu shepherd and not seen for six years. When we next hear of him he is a devil, just such a blistering devil as that gout of tortured mountain water. But he is not a jet of water, he is a human being; his explosion is not over in a second, but is to go on for years.

"Something has happened to him in the shepherd's house in those six years, something which put the cover down tight over what was in him, and heated it up."

Vicente, the boy, asks, "What was it?"

Massoni says nothing for a long time, and then says he doesn't know. Says, "I mean to find out some day ... if I can. The shepherd is dead now, the wife disappeared, the other children gone, perhaps dead too. They lived alone in a rocky place, without neighbors, fishing and herding sheep and perhaps other things . . . anyway, they are gone. All but this unhappy demon of a boy."

(I, Guido, feel a flash of rage. Who's unhappy?)

Massoni says, "So you see what can happen if a talent big enough is held back hard enough."

Vicente, the boy, says, "You mean to live apart from all music did such a thing to this child?"

Massoni shakes his head, says, "No, that would not be enough by itself. It must have been something more —something that was done to him, and done so thoroughly that this has happened."

"What things does he do?"

"Cruel, vicious things. They say meaningless things; but they are not meaningless. He beat an old beggar one night and broke his legs. He set fire to a print shop. He cut the hydraulic brake tube on a parked bus. He threw a big building-stone through the stained glass of St. Anthony's. He destroyed the big loud-speaker over the door of a phonograph shop with the handle of a broom. And there are dozens of small things, meaningless until one realizes the single thread that runs through them all. Knowing that, one can understand why he does these things (though not why he wants to). One can also know, in the long list of small crimes, cruelties and ruinations a city like this must write each day, each week, which are done by this unfortunate boy and which are not."

"Has no one seen him?" asks Vicente.

"Hardly. He took a toy from a child and smashed it under his foot, and we got a description; but it was a five-year-old child, it was after dark, it happened very quickly; it was not evidence enough to hold him.

There was a witness when he wrecked the loud-speaker, and when he pushed a porter's luggage-truck on to the tracks at the railroad station, but again it was dark, fast, confused; the witnesses argued with one another and he went free. He moves like the night wind, appears everywhere, strikes when he is safe and the act is unexpected."

(Ah now, Massoni, you are beginning to tell the truth.)

The boy Vicente wants to know how one may be sure all these things are really the work of this one boy.

Massoni says, "It is the thread that runs through all his acts. In the shrine, St. Anthony's, a choir was practicing. The toy he smashed was a harmonica. On the luggage truck were instrument cases, a trombone and a flügelhorn. The damaged bus carried members of an orchestra and their instruments (and a driver who had his wits about him, tried his brakes even as he began to move, or all might have been killed). The destruction of the loud-speaker speaks for itself. Always something about music, something against music."

"The beggar?"

"A mad old man who sang all the time. You see?"

"Ah," says the boy Vicente sadly.

"Yes, it is a sad thing. If music angers him so, his days and his nights must be a furnace of fury, living as he does in the most musical land on earth, with every voice, whistle, bell, each humming, singing, plunking, tinkling man, woman and child reaching him with music . . . music reaches him, you see, as nothing can reach you and me, Vicente; it reaches him more than rain; it splashes on his heart and bones. . . . Ah, forgive me, forgive me, boy; I am using your lesson time on a matter of police business. Yet—it is not time wasted, if you gain from it something about the nature of talent, and how so natural a thing can break a block of stone to thrust one tender shoot into the sun, as you have seen a grass-blade do. And remember, too, that a great talent is not a substitute for work. A man of small skill, or even good skill like mine, must practice until his fingers bleed to bring his talent to flower; but if your talent is great, why then you must work even harder. The stronger the growth, the more tangled it can become; we want you to make a tall tree and not a great wide bramble-patch. Now enough of talk. Take up the violin."

... So again I Guido descend into hell, while Massoni coaxes and goads the boy who goads and coaxes the instrument to scratch, squawk, squeak and weep. In between noises is advice and learning: "A little higher with the bow arm, Vicente—so; now if there is a board resting on wrist, elbow, shoulder, I may set a brimming glass there and never spill. And to this level you must always return." ... "Na, na, get the left elbow away from the body, Vicente. Nobody scrunches up arm and fingers that way to play ... except Joseph Szigeti, of course, and you are not going to be the second Szigeti but the first Vicente Pandori."

From my hole in the ceiling I Guido watch, and then strangely cease to watch ... as if watching was a thing to do, to try to do and a thing I could do or not do ... and as if I ceased trying to do this thing and became instead something not-alive, like a great gaping street-sewer, letting everything pour into me. A few minutes ago I am ready to shout, to come out, to kill—anything to stop this agony. Now I am past that. I am beaten into a kind of unconsciousness ... no; a sleep of the will;

the consciousness is open and awake as never before. Along with it a kind of blindness with the eyes seeing. I see, but I am past seeing, past understanding what I see. I do not see them finish. I do not see them go. I am, after a long time, aware of what seems to be the sound of the violin, when the big low G string is touched by one single soft bounce of the bow, scraping a little under the boy's fledgling fingers. Hearing this, over and over, I begin to see normally again, and see only the dark room with a single band of light across it from a street-lamp outside the wide slit of window. Massoni is gone. Vicente is gone. The violin is gone. Yet I hear it, that soft scraping *staccato,* over and over.

It hurts my throat.

*Hcoo ... hcoo ...*

It hurts each time, the quiet sound, as if I am the violin being struck softly, and being so tender, hurting so easily, I softly cry out. . . .

And then I understand that it is not a violin I hear; I am sobbing up there in the dark. Enraged, I swallow a mouthful of sour, and stop the noise.

# CHAPTER 5

"So—whaddaya want?"

The Medusa told him what it wanted, incredulously, as one explaining the utter and absolute obvious, and drew a blank from Gurlick. There was a moment of disbelief, and then a forceful repetition of the demand.

And Gurlick still did not understand. Few humans would, for not many have made the effort to comprehend the nature of the hive-mind—what it must be like to have such a mind, and further, to be totally ignorant of the fact that any other kind of mind could exist.

For in all its eons of being, across and back and through and through the immensities of space it occupied, the Medusa had never encountered intelligence except as a phenomenon of the group. It was aware of the almost infinite variations in kind and quality of the *gestalt* psyche, but so fused in its experience and comprehension were the concepts "intelligence" and "group" that it was genuinely incapable of regarding them as separable things. That a single entity of any species was capable of so much as lucid thought without the operation of group mechanisms, was outside its experience and beyond its otherwise near-omniscience. To contact any individual of a species was—or had been until now—to contact the entire species. Now, it pressed against Gurlick, changed its angle and pressed again, paused to ponder, came back again and, puzzling, yet again to do the exploratory, bewildered things a man might do faced with the opening of, and penetration through, some artifact he did not understand. There were tappings and listenings, and (analogously) pressures this way and that as if to find a left-hand thread. There were scrapings as for samples to analyze, proddings and pricks as for hardness tests, polarized rayings as if to determine lattice structures. And in the end there was a—call it a pressure test, the procedure one applies to clogged tubing or to oxide-shorts on shielded wire: blow it out. Take what's supposed to be going through and cram an excess down it.

Gurlick sat on the floor of the abandoned truck, disinterestedly aware of the distant cerebration, computation, discussion and conjecture. A lot of gabble by someone who knew more than he did about things he didn't understand. Like always.

*Uh!*

It had been a thing without sight or sound or touch, but it struck like all three, suffused him for a moment with some unbearable tension, and then receded and left him limp and shaken. Some mighty generator somewhere had shunted in and poured its product to him, and it did a great many things inside him somehow; and all of them hurt, and none was what was wanted.

He was simply not the right conduit for such a force. He was a solid bar fitted into a plumbing system, a jet of air tied into an electrical circuit; he was the wrong material in the wrong place and the output end wasn't hooked up to anything at all.

Spectacular, the degree of mystification which now suffused the Medusa. For ages untold there had always been some segment somewhere which could come up with an answer to anything; now there was not. That particular jolt of that particular force ought to have exploded into the psyche of every rational being on earth, forming a network of intangible, unbreakable threads leading to Gurlick and through him to Medusa itself. It had *always* happened that way—not almost always, but always. This was how the creature expanded. Not by campaign, attack, seige, consolidation, conquest, but by contact and influx. Its "spores," if they encountered any life-form which the Medusa could not control, simply did not function. If they functioned, the Medusa flowed in. *Always.*

From methane swamp to airless rock, from sun to sun through two galaxies and part of a third flickered the messages, sorting, combining, test-hypothesizing, calculating, extrapolating. And these flickerings began to take on the hue of fear. The Medusa had never known fear before.

To be thus checked meant that the irresistible force was resisted, the indefensible was guarded. Earth had a shield, and a shield is the very next thing to a weapon. It *was* a weapon, in the Medusa's lexicon; for expansion was a factor as basic to its existence as Diety to the religious, as breath or heart beat to a single animal; such a factor may not, must not be checked.

Earth suddenly became a good deal more than just another berry for the mammoth to sweep in. Humanity now had to be absorbed, by every measure of principle, of gross ethic, of life.

And it must be done through Gurlick, for the action

of the "spore" within him was irreversible, and no other human could be affected by it. The chances of another being in the same sector at the same time were too remote to justify waiting, and Earth was physically too far from the nearest Medusa-dominated planet to allow for an attack in force or even an exploratory expedition, whereby expert mind might put expert hands (or palps or claws or tenacles or cilia or mandibles) to work in the field. No, it had to be done through Gurlick, who might be—must be—manipulated by thought emanations, which are nonphysical and thereby exempt from physical laws, capable of skipping across a galaxy and back before a light-ray can travel a hundred yards.

Even while, after that blast of force, Gurlick slumped and scrabbled dazedly after his staggering consciousness, and as he slowly rolled over and got to his knees, grunting and pressing his head, the Medusa was making a thousand simultaneous computations and setting up ten thousand more. From the considerations of a space-traveling culture deep in the nebula came a thought in the form of an analogy: as a defense against thick concentrations of cosmic dust, these creatures had designed space-ships which, on approaching a cloud, broke up into hundreds of small streamlined parts which would come together and reunite when the danger was past. Could that be what humanity had done? Had they a built-in mechanism, like the chipmunk's tail, the sea-cucumber's ejectible intestines, which would fragment the hive-mind on contact from outside, break it up into two and a half billion specimens like this Gurlick?

It seemed reasonable. In its isolation as the only logical hypothesis conceivable by the Medusa, it seemed so reasonable as to be a certainty.

How could it be undone, then, and humanity's total mind restored? Therein lay the Medusa's answer. Unify humanity (it thought, reunify humanity) and the only problem left would be that of influx. If that influx could not be done through Gurlick directly, other ways might be found: it had never met a hive-mind yet that it couldn't enter.

Gasping, Gurlick grated, "Try that again, you gon' kill me, you hear?"

Coldly examining what it could of the mists of his mind, the Medusa weighed that statement. It doubted it. On the other hand, Gurlick was, at the moment, infinitely valuable. It now knew that he could be hurt, and organisms which can be hurt can be driven. It realized also that Gurlick might be more useful, however, if he could be enlisted.

To enlist an organism, you find out what it wants, and give it a little in a way that indicates promise of more. It asked Gurlick then what he wanted.

"Lea' me alone," Gurlick said.

The response to that was a flat negative, with a faint stirring of that wrenching, explosive force it had already used. Gurlick whimpered, and the Medusa asked him again what he wanted.

"What do I want?" whispered Gurlick. He ceased, for the moment to use words, but the concepts were there. They were hate and smashed faces, and the taste of good liquor, and a pile of clothes by the bank of a pond: she saw him sitting there and was startled for a moment; then she smiled and said, "Hello, Handsome." What did he want? . . . Thoughts of Gurlick striding down the street, with the people scurrying away before him in terror and the bartenders standing in their open doors, holding shot-glasses out to him, calling, pleading. And all along South Main Street, where the fancy restaurants and clubs are, with the soft-handed hard-eyed big shots who never in their lives had an empty belly, them and their clean sweet-smelling women, Gurlick wanted them lined up and he would go down the line and slit their bellies and take out their dinners by the handful and throw it in their faces.

The Medusa at this point had some considerable trouble interrupting. Gurlick, on the subject of what Gurlick wanted, could go on with surprising force for a very long time. The Medusa found it possible to understand this resentment, surely the tropistic flailing of something amputated, something denied full function, robbed, deprived. And of course, insane.

Deftly, the Medusa began making promises. The rewards described were described vividly indeed, and in detail that enchanted Gurlick. They were subtly implanted feedback circuits from his own imaginings, and they dazzled him. And from time to time there was a faint prod from that which had hurt him, just to remind him that it was still there.

At last, "Oh, sure, sure," Gurlick said. "I'll find out about that, about how people can get put together again. An' then, boy, I gon' step on their face."

So it was, chuckling, that Daniel Gurlick went forth from his wrecked truck to conquer the world.

# CHAPTER 6

Dimity Carmichael sat back and smiled at the weeping girl. "Sex," she told Caroline, "is, after all, so *unnecessary*."

Caroline knelt on the rug with her face hidden in the couch cushion, her nape bright red from her weeping, the end strands of her hair wet with tears.

She had come unexpectedly, in mid-afternoon, and Dimity Carmichael had opened the door and almost screamed. She had caught the girl before she could fall, led her to the couch. When Caroline could speak, she muttered about a dentist, about how it had hurt, how she had been so sure she could make it home but was just too sick, and, finding herself here, had hoped Dimity would let her lie down for a few minutes. . . . Dimity had made her comfortable and then, with a few sharp unanswerable questions ("What dentist? What is his name? Why couldn't you lie down in his office? He wanted you out of there as soon as he'd finished, didn't he? In fact, he wasn't a dentist and he didn't do the kind of operations dentists do, isn't that so?"), she had reduced the pale girl to this sodden sobbing thing huddled against the couch. "I've known for a long time how you were carrying on. And you finally got caught."

41

It was at that point, after thinking it out in grim, self-satisfied silence, that Dimity Carmichael said sex was after all so unnecessary. "It certainly has done you no good. Why do you give in, Caroline? You don't *have* to."

"I did, I did . . ." came the girl's muffled voice.

"Nonsense. Say you wanted to, and we'd be closer to the truth. No one *has* to."

Caroline said something—*I love* (or *loved*) *him so,* or some such. Dimity sniffed. "Love, Caroline, isn't . . . *that.* Love is everything else there can be between a man and a woman, without *that.*"

Caroline sobbed.

"That's your test, you see," explained Dimity Carmichael. "We are human beings because there are communions between us which are not experienced by—by rabbits, we'll say. If a man is willing to make some great sacrifice for a woman, it might be a proof of love. Considerateness, chivalry, kindness, patience, the sharing of great books and fine music—these are the things that prove a *man.* It is hardly a demonstration of manhood for a man to prove that he wants what a rabbit wants as badly as a rabbit wants it."

Caroline shuddered. Dimity Carmichael smiled tightly. Caroline spoke.

"What? What's that?"

Caroline turned her cheek to rest it in her clenching hand. Her eyes were squeezed closed. "I said . . . I just can't see it the way you do. I can't."

"You'd be a lot happier if you did."

"I know, I know . . ." Caroline sobbed.

Dimity Carmichael leaned forward. "You can, if you like. Even after the kind of life you've lived—oh, I know how you were playing with the boys from the time you were twelve years old—but that can all be wiped away, and this will never bother you again. If you'll let me help you."

Caroline shook her head exhaustedly. It was not a refusal, but instead, doubt, despair.

"Of course I can," said Dimity, as if Caroline had spoken her doubts aloud. "You just do as I say." She waited until the girl's shoulders were still, and until she lifted her head away from the couch, turned to sit on her calves, look sideways up at Dimity from the corners of her long eyes.

"Do what?" Caroline asked forlornly.

"Tell me what happened—everything."

"You know what happened."

"You don't understand. I don't mean this afternoon— that was a consequence, and we needn't dwell on it. I want the cause. I want to know exactly what happened to get you into this."

"I won't tell you his name," she said sullenly.

"His name," said Dimity Carmichael, "is legion, from what I've heard. I don't care about that. What I want you to do is to describe to me exactly what happened, in every last detail, to bring you to *this*," and she waved a hand at the girl, and her "dentist," and all the parts of her predicament.

"Oh," said Caroline faintly. Suddenly she blushed. "I—I can't be sure just wh-which time it was," she whispered.

"That doesn't matter either," said Dimity flatly. "Pick your own. For example the first time with this latest one. All right? Now tell me what happened—every last little detail, from second to second."

Caroline turned her face into the upholstery again. "Oh . . . why?"

"You'll see." She waited for a time, and then said, "Well?" and again, "Look, Caroline; we'll peel away the sentiment, the bad judgment, the illusions and delusions and leave you free. As I am free. You will see for yourself what it is to be that free."

Caroline closed her eyes, making two red welts where the lids met. "I don't know where to begin . . ."

"At the beginning. You had been somewhere—a dance, a club . . . ?"

"A . . . a drive-in."

"And then he took you . . ."

"Home. His house."

"Go on."

"We got there and had another drink, and—and it happened, that's all."

"*What* happened?"

"Oh, I can't, I can't talk about it! Not to you! Don't you see?"

"I don't see. This is an emergency, Caroline. You do as I tell you. Forget I'm me. Just talk." She paused and then said quietly, "You got to his house."

The girl looked up at her with one searching, pleading look, and, staring down at her hands, began speaking rapidly. Dimity Carmichael bent close to listen, and let her go on for a minute, then stopped her. "You have to say exactly how it was. Now—this was in the parlor."

"L-Living room."

"Living room. You have to see it all again—drapes, pictures, everything. The sofa was in front of the fireplace, is that right?"

Caroline haltingly described the room, with Dimity repeating, expanding, insisting. Sofa here, fireplace there, table with drinks, window, door, easy-chair. How warm, how large, what do you mean red, *what* red were the drapes? "Begin again so I can see it."

More swift and soft speech, more interruption. "You wore what?"

"The black faille, with the velvet trim and that neckline, you know . . ."

"Which has the zipper—"

"In the back."

"Go on."

She went on. After a time Dimity stopped her with a hand on her back. "Get up off the floor. I can't hear you. Get up, girl." Caroline rose and sat on the couch. "No, no; lie down. Lie down," Dimity whispered.

Caroline lay down and put her forearms across her eyes. It took a while to get started again, but at last she did. Dimity drew up an ottoman and sat on it, close, watching the girl's mouth.

"Don't say *it*," she said at one point. "There are names for these things. Use them."

"Oh, I . . . just *couldn't*."

"Use them."

Caroline used them. Dimity listened.

"But what were you feeling all this time?"

"F-Feeling?"

"Exactly."

Caroline tried.

"And did you say anything while this was going on?"

"No, nothing. Except—"

"Well?"

"Just at first," whispered the girl. She moved and was

still again, and her concealing arms clamped visibly tighter against her eyes. "I think I went . . ." and her teeth met, her lips curled back, her breath hissed in sharply.

Dimity Carmichael's lips curled back and she clenched her teeth and sharply drew in her breath. "Like that?"

"Yes."

"Go on. Did he say anything?"

"No. Yes. Yes, he said, 'Caroline. Caroline. Caroline,'" she crooned softly.

"Go on."

She went on. Dimity listened, watching. She saw the girl smiling and the tears that pressed out through the juncture of forearm and cheek. She watched the faint flickering of white-edged nostrils. She watched the breast in its rapid motion, not quite like that which would result from running up stairs, because of the shallow shiver each long inhalation carried, the second's catch and hold, the gasping release. "Ah-h-h-h!" Caroline screamed suddenly, softly. "Ahh . . . I thought he loved me, I did think he loved me!" She wept, and then said, "That's all."

"No, it isn't. You had to leave. Get ready. Hm? What did he say? What did you say?"

Finally, when Caroline said, ". . . and that's all," there were no questions to ask. Dimity Carmichael rose and picked up the ottoman and placed it carefully where it belonged by the easy-chair, and sat down. The girl had not moved.

"Now how do you feel?"

Slowly the girl took down her arms and lay looking at the ceiling. She wet her lips and let her head fall to the

46

side so she could look at Dimity Carmichael, composed in the easy-chair—a chair not too easy, but comfortable for one who liked a flat seat and a straight back. The girl searched Dimity Carmichael's face, looking apparently for shock, confusion, anger, disgust. She found none of these, nothing but thin lips, dry skin, cool eyes. Answering at last, she said, "I feel . . . awful." She waited, but Dimity Carmichael had nothing to say. She sat up painfully and covered her face with her hands. She said, "Telling it was making it happen all over again, almost real. But—"

Again a silence.

"—but it was like . . . doing it in front of somebody else. In front of—"

"In front of me?"

"Yes, but not exactly."

"I can explain that," said Dimity. "You did it in front of someone—your*self. You were watched.* After this, every time, every single time, Caroline, you will always be watched. You will never be in such a situation again," she intoned, her voice returning and returning to the same note like some soft insistent buzzer, "without hearing yourself tell it, every detail, every sight and sound of it, to someone else. Except that the happening and the telling won't be weeks apart, like this time. They'll be simultaneous."

"But the telling makes it all so . . . cheap, almost . . . funny!"

"It isn't the telling that makes it that way. The act is itself ridiculous, ungraceful, and altogether too trivial for the terrible price one pays for it. Now you can see it as I see it; now you will be unable to see it any other way. Go wash your face."

She did, and came back looking much better, with her hair combed and the furrows gone from her brows and the corners of her long eyes. With the last of her makeup gone, she looked even younger than usual; to think she was actually two years older than Dimity Carmichael was incredible, incredible. . . . She slipped on her jacket and took up her top coat and handbag. "I'm going. I . . . feel a lot better. I mean about . . . things."

"It's just that you're beginning to feel as I do about . . . things."

"Oh!" Caroline cried from the door, from the depths of her troubles, her physical and mental agonies, the hopeless complexity of simply trying to live through what life presented. "Oh," she cried, "I wish I were like you. I wish I'd always been like you!" And she went out.

Dimity Carmichael sat for a long time in the not-quite-easy chair with her eyes closed. Then she rose and and went into the bedroom and began to take off her clothes. She needed a bath; she felt proud. She had a sudden recollection of her father's face showing a pride like this. He had gone down into the cesspool to remove a blockage when nobody else would do it. It had made him quite sick, but when he came up, unspeakably filthy and every nerve screaming for a scalding bath, it had been with that kind of pride. Mama had not understood that nor liked it. She would have borne the unmentionable discomforts of the blocked sewer indefinitely rather than have it known even within the family that Daddy had been so soiled. Well, that's the way Daddy was. That's the way Mama was. The episode somehow crystallized the great difference between them, and why Mama had been so glad when he died, and how it was that Dimity's given name—given by him—was one which reflected all the luminance of wickedness and sin, and why Salomé Carmichael came to be known as Dimity from the day he died. No cesspools for her. Clean, cute, crisp was little Dimity, decent, pleated, skirted and cosy all her life.

To get from her bedroom into the adjoining bath—seven steps—she bundled up in the long robe. Once the shower was adjusted to her liking, she hung up the robe and stepped under the cleansing flood. She kept her gaze, like her thoughts, directed upward as she soaped. The detailed revelation she had extracted from Caroline flashed through her mind, all of it, in a second, but with no detail missing. She smiled at the whole disgusting affair with a cool detachment. In the glass door of the shower-stall she saw the ghost-reflection of her face, the coarse-fleshed, broad nose, the heavy chin with its random scattering of thick curled hairs, the strong square clean yellow teeth. *I wish I were like you, I wish I'd always been like you!* Caroline had said that, slim-waisted, full-breasted Caroline, Caroline with the mouth which, in relaxation, pouted to *kiss me,* Caroline with the skin of a peach, whose eyes were long jewels of a rare cut, whose hair was fine and glossy and inwardly ember-radiant. *I wish I were like you . . .* Could Caroline have known that Dimity Carmichael had yearned all her life for those words spoken that way by Caroline's kind of woman? For were they not the words Dimity herself repressed as she turned the pages of magazines, watched the phantoms on the stereophonic, technicolored, wide deep unbearable screen?

It was time now for the best part of the shower, the part Dimity looked forward to most. She put her hand on the control and let it rest there, ecstatically delaying the transcendent moment.

... *Be like you* ... perhaps Caroline would, one day, with luck. How good not to *need* all that, how fine and clear everything was without it! How laughingly revolting, to have a man prove the power of a rabbit's preoccupations with his animal strugglings and his breathy croonings of one's name, "Salomé, Salomé, Salomé ..." (I mean, she corrected herself suddenly and with a shade of panic, "Caroline-Caroline-Caroline.")

In part because it was time, and partly because of a swift suspicion that her thoughts were gaining a momentum beyond her control and a direction past her choice, she threw the control hard over to *Cold,* and braced her whole mind and body for that clean (surely sexless) moment of total sensation by which she punctuated her entire inner existence.

As the liquid fire of cold enveloped her, the lips of Dimity Carmichael turned back, the teeth met, the breath was drawn in with a sharp, explosive sibilance.

# CHAPTER 7

Gurlick sank his chin into his collarbones, hunched his shoulders, and shuffled. "I'll find out," he promised, muttering. "You jus' let me know what you want, I'll find out f'ya. Then, boy, look out."

At the corner, sprawled out on the steps of an abandoned candy store, he encountered what at first glance seemed to be an odorous bundle of rags. He was about to pass it when he stopped. Or was stopped.

"It's on'y Freddy," he said disgustedly. "He don't know nothin' hardly."

"Gah dime, bo?" asked the bundle, stirring feebly, and extending a filthy hand which flowered on the stem of an impossibly thin wrist.

"Well, sure I said somebody oughta know," growled Gurlick, "but not him, f'godsakes."

"Gah dime, bo? Oh . . . it's Danny. Got a dime on ya, Danny?"

"All right, all right, I'll ast 'im!" said Gurlick angrily, and at last turned to Freddy. "Shut up, Freddy. You know I ain't got no dime. Listen, I wanna ast you somethin'. How could we get all put together again?"

Freddy made an effort which he had apparently not

considered worth while until now. He focused his eyes. "Who—you and me? What you mean, put together?"

"I *tole* you!" said Gurlick, not speaking to Freddy; then at the mingled pressure of threat and promise, he whimpered in exasperation and said, "Just tell me can we do it or not, Freddy."

"What's the matter with you, Danny?"

"You gon' tell me or aincha?"

Freddy blinked palely and seemed on the verge of making a mental effort. Finally he said, "I'm cold. I been cold for three years. You got a drink on you, Danny?"

There wasn't anybody around, so Gurlick kicked him. "Stoopid," he said, tucked his chin down, and shuffled away. Freddy watched him for a while, until his gritty lids got too heavy to hold up.

Two blocks farther, Gurlick saw somebody else, and immediately tried to cross the street. He was not permitted to. "No!" he begged. "No, no, no! You can't ast every single one you see." Whatever he was told, it was said in no uncertain terms, because he whined, "You gon' get me in big trouble, jus' you wait."

Ask he must: ask he did. The plumber's wife, who stood a head taller than he and weighed twice as much, stopped sweeping her stone steps as he shuffled toward her, head still down but eyes up, and obviously not going to scuttle past as he and his kind usually did.

He stopped before her, looking up. She would tower over him if he stood on a box; as it was, he was on the sidewalk and she on the second step. He regarded her like a country cousin examining a monument. She looked down at him with the nauseated avidity of a witness to an automobile accident.

He wet his lips, and for a moment the moment held them. Then he put a hand on the side of his head and screwed up his eyes. The hand fell away; he gazed at her and croaked, "How can we get together again?"

She kept looking at him, expressionless, unmoving. Then, with a movement and a blare of sound abrupt as a film-splice, she threw back her head and laughed. It seemed a long noisy while before the immense capacity of her lungs was exhausted by that first great ring of laughter, but when it was over it brought her face down again, which served only to grant her another glimpse of Gurlick's anxious filthy face, and caused another paroxysm.

Gurlick left her laughing and headed for the park. Numbly he cursed the woman and all women, and all their husbands, and all their forebears.

Into the park the young spring had brought slim grass, tree buds, dogs, children, old people and a hopeful ice-cream vendor. The peace of these beings was leavened by a scattering of adolescents who had found the park on such a day more attractive than school, and it was three of these who swarmed into Gurlick's irresolution as he stood just inside the park, trying to find an easy way to still the demand inside his head.

"Dig the creep," said the one with *Heroes* on the back of his jacket, and another: "Or-*bit!*" and the three began to circle Gurlick, capering like stage Indians, holding fingers out from their heads and shrilling, "Bee-beep! bee-beep" satellite signals.

Gurlick turned back and forth for a moment like a weathervane in a williwaw, trying to sort them out. "Giddada year," he growled.

"Bee-beep!" cried one of the satellites. "Stand by fer

re-*yentry!*" The capering became a gallop as the orbits closed, swirled around him in a shouting blur, and at the signal, "Burnout!" they stopped abruptly and the one behind Gurlick dropped to his hands and knees while the other two pushed. Gurlick hit the ground with a *whoosh,* flat on his back with his arms and legs in the air. Around the scene, one woman cried out indignantly, one old man's mouth popped open with shock, and everyone else, everyone else, laughed and laughed.

"Giddada year," gasped Gurlick, trying to roll over and get his knees under him.

One of the boys solicitously helped him to his feet, saying to another, "Now, Rocky, ya shoonta. Ya shoonta." When the trembling Gurlick was upright and the second of the trio—the "Hero"—down on his hands and knees behind him again, the solicitous one gave another push and down went Gurlick again. Gurlick, now dropping his muffled pretenses of threat and counterattack, lay whimpering without trying to rise. Everybody laughed and laughed, all but two, and they didn't do anything. Except move closer, which attracted more laughers.

"Space Patrol! Space Patrol," yelled Rocky, pointing at the approaching blue uniform. "Four o'clock high!"

"Esss-*cape* velocity!" one of them barked; and with their antenna-fingers clamped to their heads and a chorus of shrill *beep-beeps* they snaked through the crowd and were gone.

"Bastits. Lousy bastits. I'll killum, the lousy bastits," Gurlick wept.

"Ah right. *Ah* right! Break it up. Move it along. Ah

right," said the policeman. The crowd broke it up immediately ahead of him and moved along sufficiently to close the gap behind, craning in gap-mouthed anticipation of another laugh . . . laughter makes folks feel good.

The policeman found Gurlick on all fours and jerked him to his feet, a good deal more roughly than Rocky had done. "Ah right, you, what's the matter with you?"

The indignant lady pushed through and said something about hoodlums. "Oh," said the policeman, "hoodlum, are ye?"

"Lousy bastits," Gurlick sobbed.

The policeman quelled the indignant lady in midprotest with a bland, "Ah right, don't get excited, lady; I'll handle this. What you got to say about it?" he demanded of Gurlick.

Gurlick, half suspended from the policeman's hard hand, whimpered and put his hands to his head. Suddenly nothing around him, no sound, no face, pressed upon him more than that insistence inside. "I don't care there *is* lotsa people, don't make me ast now!"

"What'd you say?" demanded the policeman truculently.

"A'right! A'right!" Gurlick cried to the Medusa, and to the policeman, "All I want is, tell me how we c'n get together again."

"*What?*"

"All of us," said Gurlick. "Everybody in the world."

"He's talking about world peace," said the indignant woman. There was laughter. Someone explained to someone else that the bum was afraid of the Commu-

55

nists. Someone else heard that and explained to the man behind him that Gurlick was a Communist. The policeman heard part of that and shook Gurlick. "Don't you go shootin' your mouth off around here no more, or it's the cooler for you. Get me?"

Gurlick sniveled and mumbled, "Yessir. Yessir," and sidled, scuttled, cringing away.

"Ah right. Move it along. Show's over. Ah right, there. . . ."

When he could, Gurlick ran. He was out of breath before he began to run, so his wind lasted him only to the edge of the park, where he reeled against the railing and clung there to whimper his breath back again. He stood with his hands over his face, his fingers trying to press back at that thing inside him, his mouth open and noisy with self-pity and anoxia. A hand fell on his shoulder and he jumped wildly.

"It's all right," said the indignant woman. "I just wanted to let you know, everybody in the whole world isn't cruel and mean and—and—mean and cruel."

Gurlick looked at her, working his mouth. She was in her fifties, round-shouldered, bespectacled, and most earnest. She said, "You go right on thinking about world peace. Talking about it, too."

He was not yet capable of speaking. He gulped air; it was like sobbing.

"You poor man." She fumbled in an edge-flaked patent leather pocketbook and found a quarter. She held it and sighed as if it were an heirloom, and handed it to him. He took it unnoticing and put it away. He did not thank her. He asked, "Do you know?" He pressed his temples in that newly developed compulsive gesture. "I got to find out, see? I got to."

"Find out what?"

"How people can get put back together again."

"Oh," she said. "Oh dear." She mulled it over. "I'm afraid I don't know just what you mean."

"Y'see?" he informed his inner tormentor, agonized. "Ain't nobody knows—nobody!"

"Please explain it a little," the woman begged. "Maybe there's *some*one who can help you, if I can't."

Gurlick said hopelessly, "It's about people's brains, see what I mean, how to make all the brains go together again."

"Oh, you poor man . . ." She looked at him pityingly, clearly certain that his brains indeed needed putting together again, and *Well, at least he realizes it, which is a sight more than most of us do.* "I know!" she cried. "Dr. Langley's the man for you. I clean for him once a week, and believe me, if you want to know somebody who knows about the brain, he's the one. He has a machine that draws wiggly lines and he can read them and tell what you're thinking."

Gurlick's vague visualization of such a device flashed out to the stars, where it had an electrifying effect. "Where's it at?"

"The machine? Right there in his office. He'll tell you all about it; he's such a dear kind man. He told *me* all about it, though I'm afraid I didn't quite—"

"Where's it at?" Gurlick barked.

"Why, in his office. Oh, you mean, where. Well, it's 13 Deak Street, on the second floor; look, you can almost see it from here. Right there where the house with the—"

Without another word Gurlick put down his chin and hunched his shoulders and scuttled off.

"Oh, dear," murmured the woman, worriedly, "I do hope he doesn't bother Dr. Langley too much. But then, he wouldn't; he *does* believe in peace." She turned away from her good deed and started home.

Gurlick did not bother Dr. Langley for long, and he did indeed bring him peace.

# CHAPTER 8

Mbala slipped through the night, terrified. The night was for sleep, for drowsing in the kraal with one of one's wives snoring on the floor and the goats shifting and munching by the door. Let the jungle mutter and squeak then, shriek and clatter and be still, rustle and rush and roar; it was proper that it should do all these things. It was full of devils, as everyone knew, and that was proper too. They never came into the kraal, and Mbala never went into the dark. Not until now.

*I am walking upside down,* he thought. The devils had done that. The top of him had forgotten how to see, and his eyes stretched round and protuberant against the blackness. But his feet knew the trail, every root and rock of it. He sidled, because somehow his feet saw better that way, and his assegai, poised against—what?— was more on the ready.

His assegai, blooded, honorable, bladed now for half its length . . . he remembered the day he had become a man and had stood stonily to receive it, bleeding from the ceremony, sick from the potions which had been poured into him and which, though they bloated his stomach, did nothing to kill the fire-ants of hunger that crawled biting inside him. He had not slept for two nights and a day, he had not eaten for nearly a week, and yet he could remember none of these feelings save as detached facts, like parts of a story told of someone else. The single thing that came to him fine and clear was his pride when they pressed his assegai into his hand and called him man. His slender little assegai, with its tiny pointed tip, its long unmarked shaft. He thought of it now with the same faint leap of glory it always brought him, but there was a sadness mixed with it now, and an undertone of primal horror; for although the weapon which slanted by his neck now was heavy steel, beautiful with carvings, it was useless ... useless ... and he was less of a man than that young warrior with his smooth tipped stick, he was less of a man than a boy was. In the man's world the assegai was never useless. It might be used well or ill, that was all. But this was the devil's world, and the assegai had no place or purpose here save to comfort his practiced hand and the tight-strung cords of his ready shoulder and back. It became small comfort, and by the moment smaller, as he realized its uselessness. His very manhood became a foolishness like that of old Nugubwa, whose forearm was severed in a raid, who for once did not die but mended, and who carried the lost limb about with him until there was nothing left of it but a twisted bundle like white sticks.

A demon uttered a chattering shriek by his very ear and scampered up into the darkness; the fright was like a blaze of white light in his face, so that for long seconds the night was full of floating flashes inside his eyeballs. In the daytime such a sound and scamper meant only the flight of a monkey; but here in the dark it meant

60

that a demon had taken the guise of a monkey. And it broke him.

Mbala was frozen in the spot, in the pose of his fright, down on one knee, body arched back and to the side, head up, assegai drawn back and ready to throw at the source of his terror. And then—

He slumped, wagged his head foolishly, and climbed to his feet like an old old man, both hands on the staff of the spear and its butt in the ground. He began to trudge forward, balanced no longer on the springs of his toes, no longer sidewise and alert, but walking flat-footed and dragging his assegai behind him like a child with a stick. His eyes had ceased to serve him so he closed them. His feet knew the way. Beside him something screamed and died, and he shuffled past as if he had heard nothing. He dimly realized that he was in some way past fear. It was not any kind of courage. It was instead a stupidity marching with him like a ring of men, a guard and a barrier against everything. In reality it was a guard against nothing, and a gnat or a centipede would penetrate it quite as readily as a lion. But through such a cordon of stupidity, Mbala could not know that, and so he found a dim content. He walked on to his yam patch.

With Mbala's people, the yam patch was a good deal more than a kitchen garden. It was his treasure, his honor. His women worked it; and when it yielded well and the bellies of his kin were full, a man could pile his surplus by his door and sit and contemplate it, and accept the company of the less fortunate who would come to chat, and speak of anything but yams while the yearning spittle ran down their chins; until at last he deigned to give them one or two and send them away praising him; or perhaps he would give them nothing, and at length they would leave, and he could sense the bitter curses hiding in the somber folds of their impassive faces, knowing they could sense the laughter in his own.

Tribal law protecting a man's yam patch was specific and horrifying in its penalties, and the tabus were mighty. It was believed that if a man cleared a patch and cultivated it and passed it on to his son, the father's spirit remained to watch and guard the patch. But if a man broke some tabu, even unknowingly, a devil would drive away the guardian spirit and take its place. That was the time when the patch wouldn't yield, when the worms and maggots attacked, when the elephant broke down the thorn trees . . . and when the grown yams began to disappear during the night. Obviously no one but a demon could steal yams at night.

And so it was that misfortune, grown tall, would mount the shoulders of misfortune. A man who lost yams at night was to be avoided until he had cleansed himself and propitiated the offended being. So when Mbala began to lose yams at night, he consulted the witch doctor, who at considerable cost—three links of a brass chain and two goats—killed a bird and a kid and did many mumbling things with stinking smokes and bitter potions and spittings to the several winds, and packed up his armamentarium and hunkered down to meditate and at last inform Mbala that no demon was offended, except possibly the shade of his father, who must be furious in his impotence to guard the yams from, not a devil, but a man. And this man must be exorcized not by devil's weapons but by man's. At news of this, Mbala took a great ribbing from Nuyu, his uncle's second son. Nuyu had traveled far to the east and had sat in the compound of an Arab trader, and had seen many wonders and had come back with a lot less respect than a man should have for the old ways. And Nuyu said among howls of laughter that a man was a fool to pay a doctor for the doctor's opinion that the doctor could not help him; he said that he, Nuyu, could have told him the same thing for a third the price, and any unspoiled child would have said it for nothing. Others did not—dared not—laugh aloud like Nuyu, but Mbala knew well what went on behind their faces.

Well, if a man stole his yams at night, he must hunt the man at night. He failed completely to round up a party, for though they all believed the doctor's diagnosis, still night marches and dealings with demon's work—even men doing demon's work—were not trifles. It was decided after much talk that this exorcism would bring great honors to anyone so brave as to undertake it, so everyone in the prospective hunting party graciously withdrew and generously left the acquisition of such honors to the injured party, Mbala. Mbala was thereby pressured not only into going, but also into thanking gravely each and every one of his warrior friends and kinsmen for the opportunity. This he did with some difficulty, girded himself for battle, and was escorted to the jungle margin at evening by all the warriors in the kraal, while his wives stood apart and wept. The first three nights he spent huddled in terror in the tallest solid crotch he could find in the nearest tree out of sight of the kraal, returning each day to sit and glower so fiercely that no one dared ask him anything. He let them think he had gone each night to the

63

patch. Or hoped they thought that. On the fourth morning he climbed down and turned away from the tree to be greeted by the smiling face of his cousin Nuyu, who waved his assegai and walked off laughing. And so at last Mbala had to undertake his quest in earnest. And this was the night during which the demons scared him at last into the numbness of impenetrable stupidity.

He reached his patch in the blackest part of the night, and slipped through the thorns with the practiced irregular steps of a modern dancer. Well into the thickest part of the bush which surrounded his yams—a bush his people called *makuyu* and others astralagus vetch— he hunkered down, rested his hands on his upright spear and his chin on his forearms. So he was here—splendid. Bad luck, thievery, shame and stupidity had brought him to this pinnacle, and now what? Man or devil, if the thief came now he would not see him.

He dozed, hoping for some lightening of the leaden sky, for a suspicious sound, for anything that would give him a suggestion of what to do next. He hoped the demons could not see him crouched there in the vetch, though he knew perfectly well they could. He was stripped of his faith and his courage; he was helpless and he did not care. His helplessness commanded this new trick of stupidity. He hid in it, vulnerable to anything but happily unable to see out. He slept.

His fingers slipped on the shaft of the assegai. He jolted awake, peered numbly around, yawned and let the weapon down to lie across his feet. He hooked his wide chin over his bony updrawn knees, and slept again.

# CHAPTER 9

"You Doctor Langley?"

The doctor said, "Good God."

Dear kind man he might be to his cleaning lady, but to Gurlick he was just another clean man full of knowledges and affairs which Gurlick wouldn't understand, plus the usual foreseeable anger, disgust and intolerance Gurlick stimulated wherever he went. In short, just another one of the bastits to hate.

Gurlick said, "You know about brains?"

The doctor said, "Who sent you here?"

"You know what to do to put people's brains together again?"

"What? Who are you? What do you want anyway?"

"Look," said Gurlick, "I got to find this out, see. You know how to do it, or not?"

"I'm afraid," said the doctor icily, "that I can't answer a question I don't understand."

"So ya *don't* know anything about brains."

The doctor sat tall behind a wide desk. His face was smooth and narrow, and in repose fell naturally into an expression of arrogance. No better example in all the world could have been found of the epitome of everything Gurlick hated in his fellow-man. The doctor was archetype, coda, essence; and in his presence Gurlick was so unreasonably angry as almost to forget how to cringe.

"I didn't say that," said Langley. He looked at Gurlick steadily for a moment, openly selecting a course of action: Throw him out? Humor him? Or study him? He observed the glaring eyes, the trembling mouth, the posture of fear-driven aggressiveness. He said, "Let's get something straight. I'm not a psychiatrist." Aware that this creature didn't know a psychiatrist from a CPA, he explained, "I mean, I don't treat people who have problems. I'm a physiologist, specializing on the brain. I'm just interested in how brains do what they do. If the brain was a motor, you might say I am the man who writes the manual that the mechanic studies before he goes to work. That's all I am, so before you waste your own time and mine, get that straight. If you want me to recommend somebody who can help you with whatev—"

"You tell me," Gurlick barked, "you just tell me that one thing and that's all you got to do."

"What one thing?"

Exasperated, adding his impatience with all his previous failures to his intense dislike of this new enemy, Gurlick growled, "I tole ya." When this got no response, and when he understood from the doctor's expression that it would get no response, he blew angrily from his nostrils and explained, "Once everybody in the world had just the one brain, see what I mean. Now they's all took apart. All you got to tell me is how to stick 'em together again."

"You seem to be pretty sure that everybody—how's that again?—had the same brain once."

Gurlick listened to something inside him. Then, "Had to be like that," he said.

"Why did it have to be?"

Gurlick waved a vague hand. "All this. Buildin's. Cars, cloe's, tools, 'lectric, all like that. This don't git done without the people all think with like one head."

"It did get done that way, though. People can work together without—thinking together. That is what you mean, isn't it—all thinking at once, like a hive of bees?"

"Bees, yeah."

"It didn't happen that way with people, believe me. What made you think it did?"

"Well, it did, thass all," said Gurlick positively.

A startled computation was made among the stars, and, given the axiom which had proved unalterably and invariably true heretofore, namely, that a species did not reach this high a level of technology without the hive-mind to organize it, there was only one way to account for the doctor's incredible statement—providing he did not lie—and Gurlick, informed of this conclusion, did his best to phrase it. "I guess what happened was, everybody broke all apart, they on their own now, they just don't remember no more. I don't remember it, you don't remember it, that one time you and me and everybody was part of one great big brain."

"I wouldn't believe that," said the doctor, "even if it were true."

"Sure not," Gurlick agreed, obviously and irritatingly taking the doctor's statement as a proof of his own.

"Well . . . I still got to find out how to stick 'em all together again."

"You won't find it out from me. I don't know. So why don't you just go and—"

"You got a machine, it knows what you're thinkin'," said Gurlick suddenly.

"I have a machine which does nothing of the kind. Who told you about me, anyway?"

"You show me that machine."

"Certainly not. Look, this has been very interesting, but I'm busy and I can't talk to you any more. Now be a good—"

"You got to show it to me," said Gurlick in a terrifying whisper; for through his fogbound mind had shot his visions (she's in the water up to her neck, saying, *Hello, Handsome,* and he just grins, and she says, *I'm coming out,* and he says, *Come on then,* and slowly she starts up toward him, the water down to her collarbone, to her chest, to—) and a smoky curl of his new agony; he had to get this information, he *must.*

The doctor pressed himself away from his desk a few inches in alarm. "That's the machine over there. It won't make the slightest sense to you. I'm not trying to hide anything from you—it's just that you wouldn't understand it."

Gurlick sidled over to the equipment the doctor had pointed to. He stood looking at it for a moment, flashing a cautious ratlike glance toward the doctor from time to time, and pulling at his mouth. "What you call this thing?"

"An electroencephalograph. Are you satisfied?"

"How's it know what you're thinkin'?"

"It doesn't. It picks up electrical impulses from a

brain and turns them into wavy lines on a strip of paper."

Watching Gurlick, the doctor saw clearly that in some strange way his visitor was not thinking of the next question; he was waiting for it. He could see it arrive.

"Open it up," said Gurlick.

"What?"

"Open it. I got to look at the stuff inside it."

"Now look here, I—"

Again that frightening hiss: "I got to see it."

The doctor sighed in exasperation and pulled open the file drawer of his desk. He located a manual, slapped it down on the desk, leafed through it and opened it. "There's a picture of it. It's a wiring diagram. If it makes any sense to you it'll tell you more than a look inside would tell you. I hope it tells you that the thing's far too complicated for a man without train—"

Gurlick snatched up the manual and stared at it. His eyes glazed and cleared. He put the manual down and pointed. "These here lines is wires?"

"Yes."

"This here?"

"A rectifier. It's a tube. You know what a tube is."

"Like radio tubes. Electric is in these here wires?"

"This can't mean anyth—"

"What's this here?"

"Those little lines? Ground. Here, and here, and over here the current goes to ground."

Gurlick placed a filthy fingertip on the transformer symbol. "This changes the electric. Right?"

Dumfounded, Langley nodded. Gurlick said, "Regular electric comes in here. Some other kind comes in here. What?"

"That's the detector. The input. The electrodes. I mean whatever brain the machine is hooked up to, feeds current in there."

"It ain't very much."

"It ain't," mimicked the doctor weakly, "very much."

"You got one of those strips with the wavy lines?"

Wordlessly the doctor opened the drawer, found a trace, and tossed it on top of the diagram. Gurlick pored over it for a long moment, referring twice to the wiring diagram. Suddenly he threw it down. "Okay. Now I found out."

"You found out what?"

"What I wanted."

"Will you be kind enough to tell me just what you found?"

"God," said Gurlick disgustedly, "how sh'd I know?"

Langley shook his head, suddenly ready to laugh at this mystifying and irritating visitation. "Well, if you've found it, you don't have to stick around. Right?"

"Shut up," said Gurlick, cocking his head, closing his eyes. Langley waited.

It was like hearing one side of a phone conversation, but there was no phone. "How the hell I'm supposed to do *that?*" Gurlick demanded at one point, and later, "I gon' need money for anything like that. No, I can't. I can't, I tell ya; you just gon' git me in th' clink. . . . What you think he's gon' be doin' while I take it?"

"Who are you talking to?" Langley demanded.

"I dunno," said Gurlick. "Shut up, now." He fixed his gaze on the doctor's face, and for seconds it was unseeing. Then suddenly it was not, and Gurlick spoke to him: "I got to have money."

"I'm not giving any handouts this season. Now get out of here."

Gurlick, showing all the signs of an unwelcome internal goading, came around the desk and repeated his demand. As he did so, he saw for the very first time that Doctor Langley sat in a wheel chair.

That made all the difference in the world to Gurlick.

# CHAPTER 10

Henry was tall. He stood tall and sat tall and had a surprisingly adult face, which made him all the more ridiculous as he sat through school day after day, weeping. He did not cry piteously or with bellows of rage and outrage, but almost silently, with a series of widely spaced, soft, difficult sniffs. He did what he was told (*Get in line . . . move your chairs, it's story time . . . fetch the puzzles . . . put away the paints*) but he did not speak and would not play or dance or sing or laugh. He would only sit, stiff as a spike, and sniff. Henry was five and kindergarten was tough for him. Life was tough for him. "Life is tough," his father was fond of saying, "and the little coward might as well learn."

Henry's mother disagreed, but deviously. She lied to everyone concerned—to her husband, to Henry's teacher, to the school psychologist and the principal and to Henry himself. She told her husband she was shopping in the mornings but instead she was sitting in the corner of the kindergarten room watching Henry crying. After two weeks of this the psychologist and the principal corralled her and explained to her that the reality of home involved having her at home, the reality of school involved *not* having her at school, and

Henry was not going to face the reality of school until he could experience it without her. She agreed immediately, because she always agreed with anyone who had a clear opinion about anything, went back to the room, told the stricken Henry that she would be waiting just outside, and marched out. She completely overlooked the fact that Henry could see her from the window, see her walk down the path and get into her car and drive away. If he had any composure left after that it was destroyed after a few minutes when, having circled the block and concealed her car, she crept back past the *Keep Off the Grass* sign, and spent the rest of the morning peeping in the window. Henry saw her right away, but the teacher and the principal didn't catch on to it for weeks. Henry continued to sit stiffly and hiss out his occasional sobs, wondering numbly what there was about school so terrifying as to make his mother go to such lengths to protect him, and, whatever it was, feeling a speechless horror of it.

Henry's father did what he could about Henry's cowardice. It pained him because, though he was certain it didn't come from his side, other people might not know that. He told Henry ghost stories about sheeted phantasms which ate little boys and then sent him up to bed in the dark, in a room where there was a hot-air register opening directly into the ceiling of the room below. The father had troubled to spread a sheet over the register and when he heard the boy's door open and close, he shoved a stick up through the register and moaned. The white form rising up out of the floor elicited no sound or movement from Henry, so the father went upstairs, laughing to see the effect he had not heard. Henry stood as stiff as ever, straight and tall, motionless in the dark, so his father turned on the light and looked him over, and then gave him a good whaling. "Five years old," he told the mother when he got back downstairs, "and he wets his pants yet."

He jumped out shouting at Henry from around corners and hid in closets and made animal noises and he gave him ruthless orders to go out and punch eight- and ten-year-olds in the nose and warmed his seat for him when he refused, but he just couldn't seem to make the dirty little sissy into anything else. "Blood will tell," he used to say knowingly to the mother who had never stood up to anyone in her life and had manifestly tainted the boy. But he clung to the hope that he could do something about it, and he kept trying.

Henry was afraid when his parents quarreled, because the father shouted and the mother wept; but he was afraid when they did not quarrel too. This was a special fear, raised to its peak on the occasions when the father spoke to him pleasantly, smiling. Undoubtedly the father himself did not realize it, but his pattern for punishing the boy was invariably a soft-voiced, smiling approach and a sudden burst of brutality, and Henry had become incapable of discriminating between a genuine pleasantry and one of these cheerful precursors to punishment. Meanwhile his mother coddled and cuddled him secretly and unsystematically, secretly violated his father's deprivations by contrabanding to him too much cookies and candy, yet all the while turned a cold and unresponsive back to any real or tacit plea for help in the father's presence. Henry's natural curiosity, along with his normal rebelliousness, had been thoroughly excised when they first showed themselves in his second and third years, and at five he was so thoroughly trained that he would take nothing not actually handed to him by a recognized authority, go nowhere and do nothing unless and until clearly instructed to do so. Children should be seen and not heard. Do not speak unless spoken to. "Why didn't you poke that kid right in the nose? Why? *Why?*"

"Daddy, I—"

"Shaddup, you little yellow-belly. I don't want to hear it."

So tall little, sad little Henry sat sniffing in kindergarten, and was numbly silent everywhere else.

# CHAPTER 11

After clubbing Dr. Langley with the floor-lamp, Gurlick rummaged around as ordered, and, bearing a bundle, went shopping. The Medusa permitted him to shop for himself first, quite willing to concede that he knew the subtleties of his own matrix better than it did. He got a second-hand suit from a hockshop in the tenderloin district, and a shave and a trim at the barber college. Esthetically the improvement was negligible; socially it was enormous. He was able to get what he wanted, though none of it was easy, since he personally knew the names of none of the things he was compelled to buy. Probably the metal samples were hardest of all to acquire; he had to go into an endless succession of glassy-eyed silences before a bewildered lab supply clerk undertook to show him a periodic table of the elements. Once he had that, things moved more rapidly. By pointing and mumbling and asking and trancing, he acquired lab demonstration samples of nickel, aluminum, iron, copper, selenium, carbon and certain others. He asked for but could not afford deuterium, fournines pure tantalum, and six-nines silver. The electrical-supply houses frustrated him deeply on the matter of small-gauge wire with a square cross-section, but someone at last directed him to a jewelry-findings store and at last he had what he wanted.

By now he was burdened with a wooden crate rigged by an accommodating clerk into something approximating a foot-locker in size and shape, with a rope handle to carry it by. His destination was decided after a painful prodding session by the Medusa, which dug out of Gurlick's unwilling brain a memory that Gurlick himself had long ago let vanish—a brief and unprofitable stab at prospecting, or rather at carrying the pack for a friend who was stabbing at it, years ago. The important facet of the memory was an abandoned shack miles from anywhere, together with a rough idea of how to get there.

So Gurlick took a bus, and another bus, and stole a jeep and abandoned it, and at last, cursing his tormentors, slavering for his dream, and wailing his discomfort, he walked.

Heavy woods, an upland of scrub pine and dwarf maple, then a jagged rock ridge—that was it; and the roofless remnant of the shack like a patch of decay between and against the stained tooth-roots of the snaggly ridge.

Gurlick wanted more than water, more than food or to be left alone, Gurlick wanted rest, but he was not allowed it. Panting and sniffling, he fell to his knees and began to fumble with the ropes on his burden. He took out the mercury cells and the metal slugs and the wire and tube-sockets, and began to jumble them together. He didn't know what he was doing and he didn't have to. The work was being done by an aggregate of computing wills scattered across the heavens, partly by direct orders, partly by a semi-direct control, brain to neurone, by-passing that foggy swamp which comprised Gurlick's consciousness. Gurlick disliked the whole thing mightily, but except for a lachrymose grumble, no protest was possible. So he blubbered and slaved, and did not, could not, let up until it was finished.

When it was finished, Gurlick was released. He stumbled away from it, as if a rope under tension had tied him and was suddenly cut. He fell heavily, reared up on his elbows to blink at the thing, and then exhaustion overcame him and he slept.

When he fell asleep it was a tangle of wires and components, a stack of dissimilar metals strangely assembled, and with . . . capabilities. While he slept, the thoughts from the stars operated it, directly at last, not needing his blunt fumbling fingers. Within one of the circlets of square wire, a small mound of sand began to smoke. It rose suddenly and drifted down, rose again and drifted down, and lay finally smooth and flat. A depression of an unusual shape appeared in it. A block of Invar tumbled end over end from the small pile of metals and dropped into the sand. It slumped, melted, ran and was cast. Another piece was formed, then another, and with a swirl like the unpredictable formation of a dust-devil, the pieces whirled and fell together, an assembly. A coil of enameled copper wire rolled to the sand bed and stopped rolling . . . but continued to rotate, as its free end crawled outward to the assembly, snaked here, there, around a prong. A faint smell of burning, and the wire was spot-welded in seven places, and burned through where it was not needed.

Now Gurlick's original conglomeration began to shed

its parts, some being invisibly shoved aside, others being drawn in to join the growing aggregate. Sometimes there was a long pause as if some inhuman digestive process were going on within the growing machine; then it would shudder as if shaken more tightly together, or it would thrust out a new sub-assembly to one side, which in turn would erect a foot-high T-shaped mast which would begin to swing from side to side as if seeking. Or there would be a flurry of activity as it tried and rejected materials in rapid succession; after one such scurry, its T-headed mast aimed at the rock near-by. There was a tense moment, a flicker of violet corona discharge; a great bite appeared in the rock, and a cold cloud of rock-dust which drifted over to the new machine and was absorbed into it—traces of silver, traces of copper, and certain borosilicates.

And when it was finished, it was . . . it was what Gurlick had built. However, it bore the same relation to the original as a superheterodyne receiver does to a twenty-cent home-rigged crystal set. Like its predecessor, it began, on the instant of its completion, to build another, more advanced version of itself.

# CHAPTER 12

Tony Brevix and his wife and their four kids and the cat were moving. Tony drove the truck, a patched, rusted, flap-fendered quarter-ton panel truck with an immense transmission, a transmogrified rear end, and a little bitty motor that had rated 42 horsepower American when it was new, which was certainly not recently. In the truck were almost all of their household goods, carefully not packed in boxes, but stacked, folded, wadded and rodded down until the entire truck body was solid as a rubber brick. With Tony rode one and occasionally two of the children, who for children's mysterious reasons counted it a privilege to be subjected to the cold, the oil-smoke from the breather which came up through the holes under the floorboard, and the vehicle's strange slantwise gait as it carried its eightfold overload on only three ancient shock-absorbers. The cat did not ride in the truck, as there was no glass in the side windows.

Atty Brevix (her name, infuriatingly, was Beatitude, which made Batty and Titty and even, in the midst of an argument, Attitude) drove the station wagon, a long, hushed, low, overpowered this-year's dream-boat with lines as clean as those of a baseball bat and an appetite like a storm sewer. She drove with great skill and even greater trepidation, since she had misplaced her driver's license some weeks earlier and was convinced that this information was marked on the sides of their caravan as in neon lights. It had grown dark at the end of their second day on the road; they had taken a wrong turning and were miles away from their chosen track, although still going in the desired direction, and they began bitterly to regret their decision to make the remaining eighty miles in one jump rather than stop at a motel again. Nerves were raw, bladders acreak; two of the children were whining, two screaming, and four-year-old Sharon, who was always either talking or sleeping, blissfully slept. The cat set up a grating reiteration of one note, two of them every three seconds, while at a dead run it made the rounds of all glass areas of the station wagon, of which there were many. Every time it ran across Atty's shoulders she bit down on her back teeth until her jaw ached. The baby had wriggled clear of his lashing and was trying to stand up in the car-bed, so Atty drove with one hand on the wheel and one on his chest. Every time he sat up she pushed him down, and every time she pushed him down he screeched. In the truck Tony drove grimly, squinting through a windshield so spiderwebbed with scratches that on-coming lights made the whole thing totally opaque. Carol, five and one of the weepers, and Billy, eight and a whiner, were the pair privileged to ride the truck, and while Billy described in incessant detail the food he wasn't getting, Carol cried steadily. It was a monotone bleat, rather like that of the cat, from whom she had probably learned it, and denoted no special sorrow but only an empty stomach. She would cease it completely at the first loom of light from an oncoming car, and announce the obvious: "Here comes another one. Summon a *bish*. Summon a *bish*."

And Billy would cease his listings ("Why *can't* I have a chocklit maltit? I bet I could drink three chocklit maltits. I bet I could drink four chocklit maltits. I bet I could drink five . . .") to say, "Carol shoon't say summon a bish, Pop. Hey, *Pop!* Carol's sayin' summon a bish."

And Tony would say, "Don't say that, Carol," whereupon the lights of the oncoming vehicle would be upon him, and in dedicated attention he would slit his eyes, set his jaw, and say precisely what Carol was trying to repeat.

Tony led, the car followed, it being somehow the male responsibility to find the right road. (They were not on the right road.) For some time he had been aware of the station wagon's headlights flashing on and off in his rear-view mirror. Each time he noticed it he cheerily flashed his own lights in acknowledgment, and kept going. After about an hour, the station wagon whisked by him like a half-heard insult and pulled in front, glaring at him with angry brake-lights. He did his best to stop in time, but Atty, though an excellent driver, had overlooked the detail of the load he was carrying, and the fact that stopping the wheels of the truck, and stopping the truck itself, were consecutive and not concurrent circumstances. In short, he ran into the back of the station wagon.

There was a moment of total cacophony. Tony closed his eyes, covered his ears, and let it pass him. He was then aware of an urgent tugging at his sleeve, and "Pop! Pop!"

82

"Yes, Billy. Carol, shut up a minute." Carol was wailing.

"You run into the station wagon, Pop."

"I noticed that," said Tony with heroic control.

"Pop . . ."

"Yes, Billy."

"Why did you run into the station wagon?"

"Just felt like it, I guess." He got out. "You stay here and see if you can make Carol happy."

"Okay, Pop." To Carol, "Shut up, mudface." Carol's wail became an angry screech. Tony sighed and walked to the front of the truck. There was no breakage, just "Bendage," he murmured, and walked up to the driver's side of the station wagon. Atty was unpinning the baby. He thumped on the window and she rolled it down. She said something but he couldn't hear it. The noise in there was classic.

"What?" he shouted.

"I said, why didn't you stop?"

He glanced back vaguely at the crumpled front end of the truck. "I *did*."

"Here, hold him." He held the baby under the armpits while she relieved him of several soggy fabrics. "You might have killed all of us. Would you believe it, Sharon's still asleep. What do you think I was blinking my lights for?"

"I thought you just wanted to say hello."

"I told you at the gas station to find some place along the road to stop so we could eat. Now everything's cold. Linda, you're six years old so *stop* that yelling!"

"What do you mean cold?"

"Our *din*ner. There's a sweet big boy, now you feel *much* better." The baby screamed *much* louder.

"I didn't know we had any dinner. You must've bought it while I had Carol in the men's room. What'd you want me to take her in the men's room for anyway? It was awful. There was a guy pounding on the—"

"Hey, Mom!" This from Billy, who had ranged up behind Tony. "You know what? Pop ran spang into the station wagon!"

"Get back in the truck."

"Stay here, Billy. It's Sharon's turn to ride in the truck anyway. We're going to eat right here, right now."

"Aw, gee, I didn't get to ride but a little tiny bit. Did you buy some choclit maltits, Mom? I bet I could drink seven—"

"Gosh, honey," said Tony, "let's go on at least until we find a place with some hot coffee and—"

"Is there a bathroom here?" demanded Linda at the top of her voice. "I got to—"

"Yeh, and a bathroom," finished Tony.

"I will not drive another inch with this hungry baby and these screaming children and my *back* hurts."

"Well, I say let's go on," said Tony firmly, and then wheedled, "Come on, honey. You know you'll be glad you did."

At that moment the cat, having reversed his orbit, caromed off the windshield and shot out the window as if he had been launched with boosters.

"You win," said Tony. "It'll take an hour to round him up. Where's that dinner?"

"Right here," said Atty composedly. She reached back of the seat and "*Oh!*"

She gingerly lifted out a square white cardboard box and opened it. Tony said, "What did you get?"

"Cheeseburgers," said Atty in stricken tones, "two

with catchup and relish. Milk. Tomato juice. Dill pickles. Black coffee and rice pudding. And"—she peered down—"blueberry pie. Here, dear. I'm not hungry."

Tony thrust his head in a little farther and, in the glow from the dome light, gazed into the box. It took a moment for his eyes to orient, as sometimes happens with an unexpected close-up on a TV screen: what *is* that? and then he found himself looking down on what looked like the relief map of some justifiably forgotten, unwanted archipelago. In a sea of cold curdled milk and tomato juice was a string of hamburger islands on whose sodden beaches could be seen the occasional upthrust prow of a wrecked and sunken dill pickle. Just under the surface blueberries bobbed, staring up at him like tiny cataracted eyeballs. Over to the northeast, a blunt island of rice pudding gave up its losing battle and, before his eyes, disappeared under the waves.

"I'm not hungry either," Tony said. Atty looked at him and tears started from her lids.

"I put it on edge," she said, tapping the limp box. "It seemed to take up so much room lying flat." And suddenly she began to laugh.

"Whatcha got? Whatcha got?" demanded Billy, and when, wordless, his father had brought out the box, he happily plunged in with both grimy hands. "Boy, oh boy, pickles. . . ."

They left it with him and began the complex process of getting the company's bladders wrung out in the roadside bushes.

The four-year-old, Sharon, woke contentedly in the back of the station wagon. She unwound her blanket and stretched. She was content; it had been a happy dream. She couldn't remember it, but it must have been a happy one because of the way she felt now. She lay drowsily listening to sounds near and far.

A wild scream, and "Mommy! Mom-*meeee!* Billy frowed sand on my bottom!"

"Billy!"

Protestingly, "No I din't she's a liar and I din't throw nothing I kicked it a little."

Daddy: "Honey, where's that little pack of Kleenex?"

Mommy: "Carol's got it, dear. In the bushes."

Daddy: "Are you out of your MIND? The truck registration's in there!"

"Puss-puss-puss! Here, puss . . ." Bang bang with a spoon on the cat's aluminum feeding dish.

Sharon became aware of the clean cool smell of fresh air, and the open tailgate near by. She slid silently out so that mean old Billy wouldn't see her and, clutching Mary Lou (an eyeless, naked, broken-footed, mattress-haired doll which was, above all things on earth, Sharon's most beloved), she slid into the dark bushes. "Don't be 'fraid," she told Mary Lou. "It's the *friendly* dark." She pressed on, stopped once to look back and be comforted at the beacon-like glow from the lights of the car and the truck, and then slipped over a ridge into velvety shadow, so dark that it seemed to be darkness itself that swallowed almost all sound from the road.

"Now that ol' Billy never find us," said Sharon to Mary Lou.

At the road, Atty said to Tony, "I don't feel tired, dear, just numb. Let's go all the way and get it over with."

86

"Yeah. Maybe we can slide into a dog-wagon and get a hot cup of coffee while the kids sleep."

"I wouldn't risk it," said Atty positively. "They'll sleep now and it will be quiet, and for the sake of a little quiet I can stand an empty stomach. I've had a belly full."

"Yes, dear," said Tony. "So we'll drive all the way. Next stop, the new house."

Later, in the truck, Linda said sleepily, "Isn't it Sharon's turn with me in the truck, Daddy?"

And Tony squinted into the windshield and said, "Hmm? Sharon? Oh, she slept through the whole thing."

And in the station wagon, Billy called, "Hey, Mom, where's Sharon?"

Atty said, "Shh. The baby's asleep. It's Sharon's turn to ride with Daddy. Go to sleep."

At which time Sharon stood on the ridge, turning round and round and looking for the guiding loom of lights. There was none, not anywhere but in the changing canyons of the cloudy sky where the stars peeped through. Turning and turning, Sharon lost the road, and herself was lost.

"Reely, it's the friendly dark," she shakily assured her doll. In the friendly (oh please be friendly) dark, she began to walk carefully, and after a while she heard running water.

# CHAPTER 13

When Gurlick fell asleep, the thing he had built was a tangle of components, possessing (to any trained terrestrial eye) a certain compelling symmetry and an elaborate uselessness (but how useless would a variable frequency oscillator seem to a wise bushman or a savage from Madison Avenue?); but when he awoke, the picture was different. Very different.

What Gurlick had built was not, in actuality, a matter receiver, although it acted as if such a thing were a possibility. It was, rather, a receiver and amplifier for a certain "band" in the "thought spectrum"—each of these terms being analogous and general. The first receiver, and its be-Gurlicked attachments, turned information into manipulation, and constructed from the elemental samples Gurlick had supplied it a second and much more efficient machine of far greater capacity. This in turn received and manipulated yet a third receiver and manipulator; and this one was a heavy-duty device. The process was, in essence, precisely that of the sailor who takes a heaving-line to draw in a rope which brings him a hawser. In a brief span of hours, machines were making machines to use available matter to make machines which would scout out and procure locally unavailable matter, which was returned to the site and used by other machines to make yet others, all specialized, and certain of these in immense numbers.

Gurlick came unbidden out of that dream, where he sat on the bank on the pile of clothes, shiny black and red and an edge of lacy white, and was greeted *(Hello, Handsome)* by her who so boldly (after he refused to go away) began to come up out of the water, slowly and gleaming in the sunlight, the water now down to her waist, and as she began to smile—he awoke in the midst of an incredible clanking city. Around him were row upon row of huge blind machines, spewing forth more machines by the moment: tanklike things with long snake necks and heads surrounded by a circlet of trumpets; silver balls ten feet in diameter which now and then would flick silently into the air, too fast to be believed, too silent; low, wide, massive devices which slid snaillike along roads of their own making, snouted with projectors which put out strange beams which would have been like light if they were not cut off at the far end as if by an invisible wall; and with these beams sniffing along the rocks, some of which trembled and slumped; and then there would be a movement up the beam to the machine, and from behind the machine silvery ingots were laid like eggs while fine cold dust gouted off to the side.

Gurlick awoke surrounded by this, blinking and staring stupidly. It was some minutes later that he realized where he was—atop a column of earth, ten feet in diameter and perhaps thirty feet high. All around for hundreds of yards the ground had been excavated and . . . used. At the edge of his little plateau was a small domed box which, when his eye fell on it, popped open and slid a flat bowl of hot, mushlike substance toward him. He picked it up and smelled it. He tasted it, shrugged, grunted, raised the bowl to his lips and dozed its contents into his mouth with the heel of his hand. Its warmth in his belly was soothing, then puzzling, then frightening, the way it grew. He put his hands to his belt-line, and abruptly sat down, staring at his numb and disobedient legs. Dazed, he looked out across the busy scene and saw approaching him a stilted device with endless treads for feet and a turtlelike housing, perhaps a dozen feet in diameter. It straddled his imprisoning column of earth, achieving a sort of mechanical tiptoe, and the carapace began to descend over him and all his perch like a great slow candle-snuffer. He now could not speak, nor could he sit up any longer; he fell back and lay helpless, staring up and silently screaming . . .

But as the device, its underside alive with more wriggling tool-tipped limbs than has a horseshoe crab, slowly covered him he was flooded with reassurance and promise, a special strength (its specialty: to make him feel strong but in no wise be strong) and the nearest thing to peace that he had ever known. He was informed that he was to undergo a simple operation, and that it was good, oh, good.

# CHAPTER 14

Who has sent me to Massoni, and Massoni to me, Guido? Is all my life, everything in it lost, glad, hungry, weary, furious, hopeful, hurt—is it planned to lead me to Massoni and Massoni to me? Who has curved the path he treads, all the places he has been and things he has done, to meet mine and travel it?

Why could he not be a policeman like other police, who begin with a crime and follow the criminal forward to his arrest, instead of backward and backward until the day he was born? He has asked and asked, smelling my cold, old footprints from here to Ancona and from Ancona to Villafresca and from there back and back to the house of the Corfu shepherd, Pansoni. He will find nothing there because the house is gone, Pansoni dead, the sheep slaughtered, the trail cold. But, finding nothing there, he has leaped backward in time to find me arriving there as an infant, and back and back through the orphanage and everywhere else, until he sees me carried whistling out of the bomb ruins near Anzio.

Perhaps he needs to find nothing more about me. He has found what no one else has known . . . I may not have known it myself . . . the thread that runs through all I have done. Who could have known that cutting the hard black hose by the bus wheel, stamping the old man's legs against the curbstone, throwing the kerosene rags into the print shop—all were ... acts of ... music?

I moan and hump myself backward to the dark climbing space behind the wall, and fall scrabbling down and backward to floor level. I press aside the loose plywood and stand shaking, aching in the room. I am caked with dried sweat and dirt; cold, hungry, frightened. I hobble to the door, beginning to sob again, that soft bouncing *staccato*. It frightens me more. The iron door is locked. I am still more frightened. I shake the door and then run away from it and sink down on my knees by the bed, looking up, right, left, to see what is after me.

What could be after me?

I look under the bed. It is there, the black leather cheek of the violin case. The violin is after me.

Kill it, then.

I put my hand under the bed, a thumb-tip at the bottom, fingertips at the top, just enough to hold, as if the thing were going to be hot. I draw it out. It is not hot. The sound it makes, scraping along the rough concrete floor, is like the last water shouting and belching down a drain, and when it stops I hear the strings faintly ringing.

I open a steel clasp at the side. Once I am running from someone and hide in a dark cellar; I go around a heap of fallen timbers and back into a dark corner; behind me a rat squeaks once and leaps at me and, as I duck, scratches my shoulder and neck and I hear its yellow fangs come together as it squeaks again: *squeak-click!* all at once. Now in the dark silence the clasp of the violin case squeak-clicks just the same, and I feel the same blinding flash of terror. I kneel limp by the bed, wait until the heart-thunder goes out of my ears.

I do not want to see this violin; with all my soul I do not, and like someone watching a runaway truck bear down on a dog in the street, helpless and horrified, I kneel there and watch my hands lift the case and set it on the bed, open the other two clasps, turn back the lid.

Sheep gut, horse hair, twigs and shingles.

I put out a finger, slip it under the neck, lift the violin up far enough to rest half out of the case, take away my finger and look at it. It weighs nothing. It makes a sound as I lift it, like the distant opening of a door. I look at the pegs, and they take my eye along to the scroll, down, up, around, around again, around to spin dizzily somewhere down in the shining wood. I put my hands over my face and kneel there shaking.

Guido moves like the night wind—Massoni said it himself. Guido is a natural thing, like holocaust, like hurricane, and no one knows where he will strike next. Guido fears nothing.

Then why crouch here like a fascinated bird staring into the jaws of a serpent? The violin will not bite. The violin is nothing to fear. It is mute now; it is only when it makes music that—

Is music something to fear?

Yes, oh yes.

Music is a pressure inside, welling up and ready to burst out and fill the room, fill the world; but let a note of it escape and *blam!* the hard hand of Pansoni, the Corfu shepherd, bruises the music back into the mouth, or clubs down hard on the nape, so that you pitch forward and lie with your mouth full of sand and speckles of pain dancing inside the eyeballs. Pansoni can hear music before it is born, lying like too much food just under the solar plexus; and there he will kick you before ever a note can escape. Be six years old, seven, and tend the sheep in the rocky hills, you alone with the stones and the wind and the soft filthy silly sheep; sit on a crag and sing all the notes he has crushed in his hut, and he will come without a sound and slip up behind you and knock you spinning and sliding down the mountain.

And in time you learn. You learn that to hum is to ask for that ready hard hand, to whistle a note is to be thrown out into the cold night and to cower there until daylight without a crust to eat. You feel the music rising within you and before it can sound its first syllable you look up and his bright black eyes are on you, waiting. So . . . you learn that music is fear, music is pain . . . and deep, deep underneath, waiting until you are tall as a man and almost strong as a man, music is revenge; music is anger. You understand Pansoni, why he does these things. Pansoni knows that the music in you is remarkable—that is to say, noticeable, and there is that about Pansoni which strikes down whatever is noticeable as soon as it shows itself. Pansoni will not risk rumors in the countryside of the shepherd's boy who can sing any aria from any opera, whistle an entire violin concerto after hearing it once. Pansoni is a smuggler. Pansoni and his sheep and his boy Guido cannot be seen against the brown rocks and shadows of the seaside hills, and he will naturally extinguish, in this music-dyed map on which we crawl, the mighty beacon of melody which waits in the breast and brain of his ragged, beaten Guido.

*Never look back, never look back,* and damn you, Massoni, damn you, violin, you have made me look back!

I take my hands from my face and look at the violin. It has not moved nor spoken, nor has the scroll unfurled, nor the strings loosed themselves to reach for me like tentacles. My one finger lifted it and put it so, half out of its bed. It is only obedient, and . . . and beautiful. . . .

I get to my feet. How long have I knelt there? My knee hurts, my foot is asleep. I take up the violin. It weighs nothing. My hand on its neck is at home; the smooth wood snugs down into my palm like part of the flesh. I squeeze it; it is strong and unyielding, not at all as fragile as it ought to be.

Squeezing it has brought the sound-box end close to me; I let it come and it touches my shoulder, throat, chin. Someone has intimately known the curve of my chin and left jaw; I turn my head a fraction, raise the fingerboard a fraction, and my chin and the ebony rest are one. I stand holding the violin like this for a long time, overcome with amazement, so much that there is no room for fear. I become aware of my chest, expanded as if to utter a note to be heard round the earth, my feet placed apart and ready to balance me when with my music I tilt the world. It is a sort of flight; my weight diminishes, my strength increases.

I take up the bow, thumb here, here the index and second fingers, the little finger straight and rigid and angling down as a prop to bear all the weight of the bow. Up elbow, down shoulder a bit . . . there: so if there is a plank across shoulder, elbow, wrist and a full glass on it, not a drop is spilled.

I balance there a long time, until the muscles of shoulder and back begin to pain me. It comes to me that this is the hurting of weariness but not of strain, and to me, strangely, this knowledge is a glory.

I take down the bow, I take down the violin, I stand with one in each hand looking at them. I have not made a sound with them, but I will. A door has opened and let in music. A door has opened and let out fear. I need not make a note with this instrument to discover whether or not the dead hand of Pansoni will strike. If it took a note of music to be sure, then I would not be sure; I would fear him still. I have become *that* free: it need not be tested.

Massoni has given me the lesson, Massoni has given me my freedom. I am grateful to Massoni now, and will do him this service: since the prevention of my crimes and the release of my terror of anything musical are things which come first with him (for is he not first a thinking policeman and only second a violinist?) I shall permit him to give me also his violin. Thank you, Massoni: thank you; it is a wondrous change you have brought about in Guido.

I find a stiff sharp knife among Massoni's things, and a piece of iron wire, and in time—more time than this usually takes me, but then I am not as I was—I get the door unlocked.

I put the violin in its case and put the case under my flapping old trench coat, and I take my leave of Massoni and all things which have brought him into my life. For this violin, this spout for the music which boils within me, I have exchanged all other things I have been and done.

I shall kill anyone who tries to take it away from me.

# CHAPTER 15

The spore, the "raisin" which Gurlick had eaten, had
been life or its surrogate. It had traversed space physically, bodily, and it had finished its function and its
capabilities with its invasion of Gurlick. But the trans-
fer of the life-essence of all the Medusa into all of
humanity was something that earth-built machines—
even if built on earth by others—could not accomplish.
Only life can transmit life. A very slight alteration indeed—an adjustment of isotopes in certain ionized
elements in Gurlick's ductless glands—would make the
membership of humanity in the corpus of the Medusa
a certainty. The machines now abuilding would ef-
fectively restore (the Medusa still unswervingly operated from a conviction that this was a restoration) the
unity of the human species, its hive-mind, so that each
"person" could reach, and be reached by, all persons;
but the fusion with the Medusa would be Gurlick's
special chore, and would take place on the instant that
his seed married with the ovum of a human female. As
the machine slowly closed over him, its deft limbs already performing the first of a hundred delicate manipulations, it caught up his dream and congratulated him
on it, and gave it detail and depth which his creative

poverty had never made possible to him before, so that he lived it realer than real, from the instant of approach (and a degree of anticipation which might have destroyed him had he felt it earlier) to the moments of consummation, so violent they shook the earth and sent the sky itself acrinkle with ripples of delighted color. And more: for in these tactile inventions there was no human limitation, and it was given to him to proceed again, and yet again, without exhaustion or dulling familiarity, either through the entire episode or through any smallest part of it, whether it be the thrill of seeing the clothes (shiny black and scarlet, and the tumbled frosting of lace-edged white) or the pounding, fainting climax. Always, too, was the laughing offhand promise that *any* conquest of Gurlick's would be such a peak, or a higher one; let him wallow in his dream because he loved it, but let him understand also that it was only one of many, the symbol of any, the quality of all.

So while it built its machines to fuse ("again") the scattered psyche of humanity, it got Gurlick—good—and—ready.

# CHAPTER 16

The warrior Mbala caught his thief perhaps an **hour** after he fell asleep squatting in the inky shadows of the astralagus vetch which encircled his yam patch. His assegai had fallen across his legs, and he was deep in that vulnerable torpor taught him by fear and weariness, so perhaps it really was the shade of his father, watching over the yam garden, who made the capture. Or that other powerful ghost man call Justice. Whatever the instrument, the thief walked out of the yam patch in the impenetrable dark and stepped so close to the sleeping warrior that his foot landed under the horizontal butt of Mbala's assegai. His other foot swung past the end of the shaft, and the first foot left the ground and caught the spear with its instep. The thief went flat on his face and the assegai snapped up and with great enthusiasm rapped Mbala painfully on the bridge of the nose.

In unison the two men squalled in terror, and then training dictated the outcome. The thief, who for most of his years had lifted nothing but other people's property, and that at irregular intervals, scrambled and slipped and fell flat again. Mbala, whose reflexes always placed action before conjecture, was up out of a sound sleep and a remaining cloud of stupidity-with-drawal, uttering a curdling battle screech, and plunging his assegai into his prostrate enemy's back before he was at all consciously aware. The prone man shrieked in agony, but it was the wrong shriek, as well as the wrong impact felt by Mbala's schooled hands. Apparently there had been enough stupidity left in that blazing moment to cause Mbala to handle his weapon as it lay, so that it was not the wide, long blade which presented itself to the thief's shoulders, but the bruising end of the shaft.

"Mbala! Mbala! Don't kill me! I am your brother, Mbala!"

Mbala, about to whirl his weapon end for end and settle the matter, checked himself and drove the haft down again. His prisoner, attempting to rise, fell flat again.

"Nuyu!"

"Yes, Nuyu, your own brother, your own dear brother. Let me up, Mbala! I haven't done anything to you!"

"I'm standing on a bag of yams," growled Mbala. "For that you die, Nuyu."

"No! No, you can't! I am the son of the brother of your father! Your father wants me spared!" Nuyu screamed. "Did he not turn your spear wrong-end-to when you first struck at me? Well, didn't he?" Nuyu insisted when Mbala seemed to hesitate.

Fury and disillusion made Mbala say, "My father is gone from here." He shifted suddenly, literally vaulting from his stance beside the prone man to one astride him, facing the feet, with his own heelbones pressing the fleshy part of the armpits flat to the ground. In pitch darkness it was done with amazing accuracy. In the moment when the warrior's weight was on the spear and pivoting, Nuyu uttered a short shrill scream, thinking his moment had come. As the rock-hard heels captured his armpits he grunted and arched his back and began flailing his legs.

"Uncle! Uncle! *Uncle!*"

Mbala reversed his spear at last. "Hold still," he said irritably. "You know I can't see."

"U-Un—cle!"

*"Now* you call on him. *Now* you fear the demon. *Now* you believe, eh, thief?" Mbala taunted. By touch alone, he drew the needle point across the man's kidneys, barely enough to part the skin. Nuyu squalled abominably and began to weep. "Uncle, uncle . . ." he sobbed and then abruptly was silent and motionless.

Mbala knew that trick well and was prepared for it, but when he began to see his shadow stretching away, lumping across the vetch and lost in the thorns, he forgot about trickery.

"Uncle . . ." Nuyu moaned. . . . There was a new note to his weeping; hope, was it? And something else?

Nuyu lay with his head toward the yam patch, Mbala stood with his back to it. The patch was roughly circular, with the tubers scattered randomly in it. A thick rim of the vetch bushes bordered it back to the thorns. Almost exactly at the four midpoints of the compass stood four ship's prow monoliths. The mound on which the patch lay must at one time have been an almost conical rock mount, before some forgotten cataclysm split it exactly in two, northeast to southwest, and again in two, northwest to southeast. Settling and erosion had widened the crossed canyons until they took the form which Mbala's dead father had found. In the native language the place was called Giant's Mouth, and it was said that a man's shout from the center of the yam patch could be heard for a day's journey in every direction.

"Uncle, oh uncle," Nuyu wept, with such a passion in his voice that Mbala bent curiously to look at him. He was bending his head back and up at an almost impossible angle, and his eyes strained at the roofs of their sockets. His dark face was . . . silver.

Mbala sprang away from him, whirling about in the air. He came down crouching, staring up at the silver ball which floated down the sky. It halted perhaps ten feet above the center of the yam patch and stayed motionless.

Nuyu made a sound. Mbala glanced quickly down at him and, without understanding why, without trying to, he bent and helped the other man to his feet. They stood close together, watching.

"Like a moon," Mbala murmured. He glanced at the silvered landscape and back again to the object. It had a brilliant, steady radiance, which fantastically left no after-image on the retina.

"He came," said the thief. "I called him and he came."

"It might be a demon."

"*You doubt your own father?*"

Mbala said, "Father . . ." And the sphere sank to the center of the yam patch. Then it opened.

There were doors completely around the object, all hinged at their upper edges, so that when they opened they formed a sort of awning all around the sphere. A beam of light fanned out to the north, but it was like no light Mbala had ever seen. It was mauve with flickers of green, and though the air was clear and the walls of the crossed canyons brilliantly lighted by the sphere, it was impossible to see through the beam. Not only that, but the beam did not fade or spread from the source outward, and terminated as sharply as if it played on a wall, which it did not. This odd square end of the light beam pressed outward from the ship until it reached the margin of vetch, and nosed into it. There was a sound like water over rapids, hissing, churning, crackling. There almost seemed to be something moving back up the light beam into the ship, but one could not be sure.

The light pressed slowly outward through the vetch to the edge of the surrounding thorn trees and stopped. No, not stopped. It was scything away from them, moving slowly, and the square end was adjusting itself to the encroachments and retreats of the thorn.

Where it had passed the vetch was gone, and where it had been the bare ground was powdered with a white substance unlike anything they had ever seen. After a few minutes it changed and the ground seemed moist.

"Can you doubt now?" murmured Nuyu. "Who but your father would clear your land?"

They stood in awe, watching the sphere clear the land. When it seemed reasonable to get out of its way they backed to the thorn and slipped through. If the sphere and its beam noticed them or their going, it made no sign. It just went on collecting and processing astralagus vetch, a weed with a high affinity for sele-nium. When it had all it could get from this pocket, it clicked shut, took a picture of the site, and leaped into the sky, where at ten thousand feet it switched on its

103

sensors, located another patch of vetch to the north, and flashed away after the only thing it knew how to care about—selenium, from astralagus.

Mbala and Nuyu crept cautiously out on the new ground and looked around in the paling dawnlight. Nuyu touched the ground with his hand. It was wet, and cold. He saw some of the white material in a hole and picked it up. It disappeared in his hand leaving only a few drops of water. He grunted and wiped his hand on his kilt. What was another miracle at a time like this?

Mbala was still staring at the sky. Nuyu said, "Will you kill me?"

Mbala brought his gaze down from the disappearing stars and gave it to Nuyu's face. He looked at it for a long while, and from all Nuyu could see there was no change in Mbala's expression at all; he looked at him as one will at distant lights. "I lost my father," he said at last, "because he let my yams be stolen. So I did not believe. But you believed, and he saved you, and he came back again. I will not kill you, Nuyu."

"I died," Nuyu breathed. "Nuyu the unbeliever died when he saw your father." He bent and picked up the sack of yams and extended them to Mbala.

"Nuyu the thief died," said Mbala. "The yams are yours and mine, forever in tomorrow and forever in yesterday. There has been no thief, then, Nuyu."

They went back to the kraal to tell the women they would have a lot of new work tomorrow. As Nuyu passed the witch doctor, the old man reached out unseen and touched Nuyu's kilt. Then the witch doctor held the touching hand in his other, and hugged them against his chest. What he got from Nuyu he could have

104

gotten from his mere presence. He knew that, but nevertheless he touched the kilt. The touch was a symbol the old man needed, and so he took and treasured it. He said to Mbala, "Your demon is dead, then."

At that Mbala and Nuyu smiled at one another, the devout and the convert, richly content with faith, and full of wonder.

# CHAPTER 17

Gurlick lay hooded and unaware, passive under the submicroscopic manipulations of the machine which brought his special membership in the Medusa to his seed. So he did not observe the change in the mighty operations around him, when the egg-laying snail-gaited miners drew in and darkened the snouts of light, and fell neatly apart to have their substance incorporated in other, more needed machines; and these in turn completed their special tasks and segmented and dispersed to others which still needed them, until at last there remained only the long-necked, tank-treaded, trumpet-headed ones, and enough silver spheres to carry them, in their multi-thousands, to their precisely mapped destinations. There was no provision for failure, for there would be no failure. The nature of the electroencephalograph, and of its traces, clearly showed to the transcendent science of the Medusa exactly what was lacking in the average mind which kept it from being a common mind. The net would be comparatively simple to cast and draw shut, for it found the potent base of the hive mentality alive and awaiting it, showing itself wherever humans blindly moved in the paths of other humans, purely because other humans so moved; where-ever friends apart impulsively sat down to write one another simultaneous letters, wherever men in groups (cartels, committees, mobs, and nations) divided their intelligence by their numbers and let that incredible quotient chart their course. The possible or probable nature of a human hive, once (re)established, was a question hardly explored, because it was hardly important. Once united, humanity would join the Medusa, because the Medusa always (not almost, not "in virtually every case," but *always*) infused the hives it touched.

So the factory-area rumbled to silence, and the noiseless spheres swept over the storage yard and scooped up their clusters of long-necked projectors, fell away up with them, flashed away to all the corners of earth, ready to place the projectors wherever their emanations (part sound, part something else) would reach masses of humans. They could not reach all humans, but they would reach most, and the established hive would then draw in the rest. No human would escape, none could; none would want to. Then, somewhere in this flawless, undivided, multi-skilled entity, Gurlick would plant a tiny fleck of himself, and at the instant of fusion between it and a living ovum, the Medusa would spread through it like crystallization through a supersaturated solution.

# CHAPTER 18

Sharon Brevix squatted on the dry part of a stony stream bed, dying. It was the second night, and she hadn't come to the ocean or a city or any people at all. Billy had told her that lost people just have to find a river and go downstream and they'll be all right, because all the rivers flow into the sea and there's always a town or people there. She had started downstream as soon as it was light on the first morning. It never occurred to her to stay where she was until she heard a car, because she must certainly still be near the road, and a car had to come by eventually. She did not reason that when she traveled the stream bed for the first hour and it did not bring her to the road, it must therefore be leading her away from it.

She was, after all, only four years old.

By ten in the morning she was aching hungry, and by noon it was just awful. She whimpered and stopped for a while to cry hard, but after a time she got up again and kept on. The ocean couldn't be terribly far away after a person walks so far. (It was another twelve hundred miles, but she could not know that.) In the afternoon she had slept for a while, and when she awoke she found some wild raspberries on a bush. She ate all she could find until she was stung by a yellowjacket and ran away screaming. She found her little stream again and kept on going until it was dark.

Now it was very late and she was dying. She felt better than she had, because she felt nothing at all very much, except hungry. The hunger had not diminished with her other sensations, but it had the virtue of blanketing them. Fear and cold and even loneliness were as unnoticeable, in the presence of that dazzle of hunger, as stars at noon. In the excitement of packing, and on the two days of traveling, she had eaten little, and she had rather less to fall back on than most four-year-olds, which is little enough.

It was after midnight, and her troubled sleep had long since turned into a darker and more dangerous condition. Cramped limbs no longer tingled, and the chilly air brought no more shivers. She slept squatting, with her back and side against a nook of rock. Later, she might topple over, very possibly too weak to move again at all but for some feeble squirmings. Yet—

She heard a sound, she raised her head. She saw what at first she thought was a Christmas tree ornament, a silver ball with a dangle of gewgaws under it, in midair a few inches from her face. She blinked and resolved it into something much larger, much farther away, coming down out of the night sky. She heard a snarling howl. She looked a little higher, and was able to identify the running lights of a small airplane streaking down out of the high overcast.

Sharon rose to her feet, holding the rock wall to steady herself while her congealed blood began to move. She saw the globe about to land on clear ground at the top of a knoll three miles away. She saw the airplane strike it dead center while it was still thirty feet off the ground, and then plane, globe, and cargo were a tangled, flaming ruin on the hill. She watched it until it died, and then lay down to finish her own dying.

# CHAPTER 19

Just another rash of saucer-sightings, thought the few observers, and recipients of their observations, in the brief minutes left to them to think as they had always thought. Some of the military had, in these minutes, a harrowing perplexity. Anything tracked at such speeds as the radars reported, must, with small variations, appear somewhere along an extrapolated path; the higher the speed, the finer the extrapolation. The few recordings made of the flick and flash of these objects yielded flight-paths on which the objects simply did not appear. It was manifestly impossible for them to check and drop straight to their destinations at such velocities; they did, however, and before the theoreticians could finish their redefinition of "impossible," they and all their co-workers, colleagues, acquaintances, cohabitants, heirs and assigns were relieved of the necessity to calculate. It happened so quickly, one minute a heterogenous mass of seething noncommunicants; the next, the end of Babel.

Henry, five years old, slept as usual flat on his back and face straight up, arms rigid, fists clenched under, and pinned down by his buttocks, and his ankles together. He was having a nightmare, soundlessly, of being surrounded by gentle smiling fathers, some of whom wore the masks of the other kids in his class, and storekeepers, and passing puppy dogs, but who were really just smiling fathers, dressed up and being gentle at the very verge of exploding in his face; and between him and all the fathers was a loving goddess with soft hands full of forbidden lollipops and raisin-bread peanut-butter sandwiches to be passed to little boys in the dark when they had been sent to bed without their suppers because they were little cowards; this goddess was there to care for him and protect him, but when the explosion came, with this breath or the next or the one after, the puppies and children and grocers and fathers would whisk through to him as if the goddess weren't there at all; and while they did what they would do to him, she would still be there smiling and ready with guilty lollipops, not knowing what the fathers were doing to him. . . . And under this nightmare was the color of hopelessness, the absolute certainty that to awake from it would be to emerge into it; the dream and the world were one now, fused and identical.

## CHAPTER 20

These were people, these are anecdotes, dwelt upon for their several elements of the extraordinary. But each man alive has such a story, unique unto himself, of what is in him and of its molding by the forces around him, and of his interpretations of those forces. Here a man sees a machine as a god, and there a man sees God as an argument; and another uses men's argument quite as if it were a tool, a machine of his own. For all his ability to work in concert with his fellows, and to induce some sympathy in their vibrations, man remains isolated; no one knows *exactly* how another feels. At the very climax of sensation, man approaches unconsciousness . . . unconsciousness of what? Why, of all around him; never of himself.

These were people, there are anecdotes of the night the world ended; this the night when people the world over thought their thoughts and lived their lives and at long, long last were wrong in thinking that tomorrow was the front part of today, yesterday the back, and that the way to go on was to go on as before.

This was the night, and the very moment, when Paul Sanders rose from the couch, lifted Charlotte Dunsay in his arms, and said, "Well if it isn't now, it never will be." . . .

When young Guido strode a pre-dawn Rome, his very bones aching with music and a carven miracle under his arm, waiting the ardent reach of his unshackled talent. No lover, no miser, no acolyte on earth loved money or woman or Master more than Guido loved this violin; no whelping fox or wounded water-buffalo so watchful for an enemy. . . .

When the cousins Mbala and Nuyu, the redeemed backslider and the convert, turned into a new and glorious day of faith and many yams. . . .

When Henry, who was five, lay stiffly in his bed and sniffled through a dream of smiling cruelties in a place quite like all other places to him, where he was despised. . . .

When Dimity Carmichael's dutiful alarm preceded the sunrise and she rose in her sensible cotton gown and made ready, eyes averted, to take her morning shower . . .

When Sharon Brevix entered the dusk and the dark of her second lost day without shelter or food . . .

Only motes among the millions, remarked upon for that about them which is remarkable, yet different only insofar as each is different *from,* or is different *within,* the pattern of qualities possessed two and three quarter billion living times under this sun.

## CHAPTER 21

He stood motionless with the girl in his arms, ready to put her down on the sofa; and then, without a start, without a word of wonderment, Paul Sanders set her on her feet and stood supporting her with a firm arm around her shoulders until her head cleared and she could stand alone.

There was nothing said, because there was in that moment nothing to be said. In a split second there was orientation of a transcendent nature—nothing as crude as mutual mind-reading, but an instant and permeating acknowledgment of relationships: I to you, we to the rest of the world; the nature of a final and overriding decision, and the clear necessity of instant and specific action. Together Paul Sanders and Charlotte Dunsay left her apartment. The hallway was full of people in all stages of dress—all moving wordlessly, purposefully. No one paid Charlotte, in her transparent gown, the slightest attention.

They walked to the elevator bank. She paused before it with a half dozen other people, and he opened the door of the fire stairs and sprang up them two at a time. Emerging on the roof, he went to the kiosk which sheltered the elevator motor and cables, twisted off the light padlock with one easy motion, opened the door, and entered. He had never been here before in his life; yet without hesitation he reached to the left and scooped up a five-foot slice-bar which lay across the grating, and ran with it back down the fire stairs.

Without glancing at floor numbers, he left the fire stairs on the fourth floor, turned left and ran down the hall. The last door on the right opened as he reached it; he did not glance at the old lady who held it for him, nor did she speak. He sped through a foyer, a living room, and a bedroom, opened the window at the far right and climbed out.

There was a narrow ledge on which he could barely keep his balance and carry the heavy bar as well, yet he managed it. The chief enemy of a balancing man is the poison of fear which permeates him: I'll fall! *I'll fall!* but Paul felt no fear at all. He made a rapid succession of two-inch sidewise shuffles until he reached the big eyebolt from which there thrust, out and down, the huge chain supporting one end of a massive theater marquee. Here he turned sidewise and squatted, brought his bar up over his shoulder, and, reaching down, thrust the tip through the fourth link of the chain. Then he waited.

The street below—what he could see of it—seemed at first glance to be normally tenanted, with about as many people about as one might expect at this hour of a Saturday night. But then it could be seen that nobody *strolled*—everyone walked briskly and with purpose; one or two people ran, the way they ran indicating running to, not from anything. He saw Charlotte Dunsay across the street, swinging along on her bare feet, and enter a showroom where computing machines were

116

on display. Though the place had been closed since noon, it was now open and lighted, and full of people silently and rapidly working.

There came a sound, and more than a sound, a deep pervasive ululation which seemed at first to be born in all the air and under the earth, sourceless. But as it grew louder, Paul heard it more from his left, and finally altogether from the corner of the building. Whatever was making that sound was crawling slowly up the street to take its place at the intersection, a major one where three avenues crossed. Patiently, Paul Sanders waited.

# CHAPTER 22

From his soundless nightmare, Henry soundlessly a-woke. He slid out of bed and trotted out of his room, past his parents' open door—they were awake, but he said nothing, and if they saw him, they said nothing either. Henry padded down the stairs and out into the warm night. He turned downtown at a dog-trot, and ran for three blocks south, one west, and two south. He may or may not have noticed that while the traffic lights still operated, they were no longer obeyed by anyone, including himself. Uncannily, cars and pedestrians set their courses and their speeds and held them, regardless of blind corners, passing and repassing each other without incident and with no perceptible added effort.

Henry had been aware for some time of the all but subsonic hooting and of its rapid increase in volume as he ran. When he reached the big intersection, he saw the source of the sound on the same street he ran on, but past the corner where the theater stood. It was a heavy tanklike machine, surmounted by a long flexible neck on top of which four horns, like square megaphones or speakers, emitted the sound. The neck weaved back and

118

forth, tilting the horns and changing their direction in an elaborate repetitive motion, which had the effect of adding a slow and disturbing vibrato to the sound.

Henry dashed across the street and under the side-street marquee. He came abreast of the thing just as it was about to enter the intersection. Without breaking stride, Henry turned and dove straight into the small space between the drive-spindle of the machine's tread and its carrier rollers. His blood spouted, and on it the spindle spun for a moment; the other track, still driving, caused the machine to swerve suddenly and bump up on the sidewalk under the marquee.

Paul Sanders, at the very instant the child had leapt, and before the small head and hands entered the machine's drive, leaned out and down and jammed the chisel point of his slice-bar hard through the fourth link of the chain. Plunging outward, his momentum carried the bar around the chain and, as his weight came upon it, gave the chain a prodigious twist. The eyebolt pulled out of the building wall with a screech, and the corner of the marquee sagged and then, as the weight of the chain came upon it, and Paul Sanders's muscular body with it, the marquee let go altogether and came hammering down on the machine. In a welter of loose bricks, sheet-tin, movie-sign lettering and girders, the machine heaved mightily, its slipping treads grating and shrieking on the pavement. But it could not free itself. Its long neck and four-horned head twitched and slammed against the street for a moment, and then the deep howl faded and was gone, and the head slumped down and lay still.

Four men ran to the wreckage, two of them pushing a dolly on which rode an oxyacetylene outfit. One man went instantly to work taking measurements with scale, micrometer and calipers. Two others had the torch going in seconds and fell to work testing for a portion of the machine which might be cut away. The fourth man, with abrasive rasps and a cold chisel, began investigating the dismantling of the thing.

And meanwhile, in unearthly silence and with steady determination, people passed and repassed, on foot, in cars, and went about their business. No crowd collected. Why should it? Everybody *knew*.

The entire village population, with Mbala and Nuyu at their head and the witch doctor following, were within two hundred yards of Mbala's yam patch when the thing came down from the sky. It was broad daylight here, so the ghostly-luminous moonlit effect was missing; but the shape of the projector as it dangled by invisible bonds from the sphere was unprecedented enough to bring a gasp of astonishment and fear from the villagers. Mbala stopped and bowed down and called his father's name, and all the people followed suit.

The sphere dropped rapidly to the yam patch, which, judging from the photograph taken by the selenium miner, seemed an ideal position for a projector to land, to send forth its commanding, mesmerizing waves.

The sphere set down its burden and started up again without pause, swift as a bouncing ball. The projector began its wavering bass hooting which swept out through the echoing clefts of the great split rock, rolled down upon the villagers, and silenced their chant as if it had blotted it up.

There was a moment—mere seconds—of frozen inaction, and then half the warriors turned as one man and plunged away through the jungle. The rest, and all the women and children, drew together, over four hundred of them, and poured swiftly up the slope toward the yam patch. No one said a word or made a sound; yet when they choked the space between two of the stone steeples, half the people ran into the clearing, skirting its edge, while half squatted where they were, blocking their avenue from side to side. The runners reached the north opening, filled it, and also squatted, wordless and waiting.

Directly across from the first group, in the westward opening, there was movement as one, two, a dozen, a hundred heads appeared, steadily and quietly approaching. It was the Ngubwe, neighboring villagers with whom there was a tradition, now quiescent, of wife-stealing and warfare going back to the most ancient days. Mbala's people and the Ngubwe, though aware of each other at all times, were content to respect each other's privacy and each cultivate his own garden, and for the past thirty years or so there had been room enough for everybody.

Now three openings to the rock-rimmed plateau were filled with squatting, patient natives. Even the babies were silent. For nearly an hour there was no sound but the penetrating, disturbing howl of the projector, no motion but its complex, hypnotic pattern of weavings and turnings. And then there was a new sound.

Blast after shrill blast, the angry sound approached, and the waiting people rose to their feet. The women tore their clothes to get bright rags, the men filled their lungs and emptied them, and filled them again, getting ready.

Through the open southern gateway four warriors erupted, howling and capering. Hard on their heels came a herd of furious elephants, three, four—seven—nine in all, one old bull, two young ones, four cows and two calves, distraught, angry, goaded beyond bearing. The fleeing warriors separated, two to the right, two to the left, sprinted to and disappeared in the crowds waiting there. The big bull trumpeted shrilly, wheeled, and charged to the right, only to face nearly two hundred shrieking, capering people. He swerved away, his momentum carrying him along the rock wall and to the second opening, where he met the same startling cacophony. The other elephants, all but one young bull and one of the calves, thundered along behind him, and when he drew up as if to wheel and attack the second group, he was pounded and pressed from behind by his fellows. By now quite out of his mind, he put up his trunk, turned his mighty shoulders against those who pressed him, and found himself glaring at this noisy, shining thing in the center of the clearing.

He shrieked and made for it. It moved on its endless treads, but not swiftly enough, nor far enough, nor in enough places at once to avoid the tons of hysteria which struck it. The elephants tore off its howling head and its neck in three successive broken bits, and shouldered it over on its side and then on its back. The howling stopped with deafening suddenness when the head came off, but the tracks kept treading the air for minutes after it was on its back.

Elephants were used in Berlin, too, on the machine which landed in the park near the famous zoo, though this was a more disciplined performance by trained animals who did exactly as they were told. In China a projector squatted in a cleft in the mountains under a railroad trestle, and began hooting into the wind. An old nomad with arthritis hobbled out of the rocks and pulled two spikes, shifted one rail. A half mile down the track, the engineer and fireman of a locomotive pulling a combination passenger-freight train with over four hundred people aboard, wordlessly left their posts, climbed back over the tender, and uncoupled the locomotive from the first car. There was, on the instant, a man at every handwheel on the train. It coasted to a stop, while far ahead the locomotive thundered over the edge of the trestle and was crushing the projector before the alien machine could move a foot.

In Baffin Land a group of Eskimo hunters stood transfixed, watching a projector squatting comfortably on mounded and impassable pack ice and, in the crisp air, bellowing its message across the wastes to the ears of four and possibly five widely scattered settlements. The hunters had not long to wait; high above the atmosphere a mighty Atlas missile approached, and, while still well below their horizon, released a comparatively tiny sliver, the redoubtable Hawk. The little Hawk came shrieking out of the upper air, made a wide half-circle to kill some of its excess velocity, and then zeroed in on the projector with the kind of accuracy the old-time Navy bombardiers would brag about: "I dropped it right down his stack."

From then on missiles got most of the projectors, though in crowded areas, other means were found. In Bombay a projector took its greatest toll—one hundred

123

and thirty-six, when a mob simply overran one of the machines and tore it to pieces with their bare hands. And in Rome one man despatched four of them and came out of it unscathed.

(A man?)

(Unscathed?)

## CHAPTER 23

I am Guido, walking the back ways and the dark paths leading out of the city, to a place where this glossy glory of a violin can make itself known to me. No human soul will hear me coax a squeak out of it, or I will kill him for knowing of it. I will kill anyone who harms it, or who tries to take it from me. This city will no longer know Guido or see Guido, and it must get along for a while without Guido's small protests against music. Against music . . . Listen now, someone is singing under the sliver of moon, far away, a little drunk. . . . No, God, that's the shift whistle at the auto place. Now wait, wait, stop and listen . . .

I stop and look down the hill, across to the other hill, and I listen as I have never listened before, and I make a great finding, one of those large things you come to know while realizing that others have always known it. How many, many times have I heard a man say wind *sings* in the wires, a *musical* waterfall, the *melody* in certain laughter. But in fighting music all these years, I have not known, I have not let myself hear all these words, nor the music which is their meaning.

I hear it now, because through owning this violin, something has happened to me. I hear the city singing while it sleeps, and I hear a singing which would sweetly cry among these hills if the city had never existed, and will cry here when it is gone.

It is as if I have new ears, yes, and a new mind and heart to go with them. I think, in the morning, when this world wakes, oh, I shall hear, I shall hear . . . and I lose the thought for its very size, thinking about what I am to hear from now on.

I go on to my hiding place. Guido's studio, I think, laughing. When they built the new highway into the city, they cut away the end of a crooked, narrow little street which used to climb the hill. Right at the top were two small houses, built Italian land style, four square stone walls which they filled with earth, then lay a four-sided dome of plaster on the earth, then dug away the earth when the plaster was hardened. These little houses will stand for a thousand years. The two I know of were buried by the embankment of the new road, where it comes near the hilltop on its stilts and curves across to the other hill. I found the houses when I escaped once from the police. I leaped from the police car and off the road, and down the embankment I put my leg in a hole, and the hole was a window. The second house is behind the first, buried completely, but there is a door between them. Two rooms in a hillside, and nobody knows but Guido.

I walk the new road, where it sweeps up to the hilltop, looking out over the city and hearing the city sing, and hearing that other music which will play, city or not, and it is all for me, for Guido. There is one thing which is not changed now: the world has always been against Guido, or Guido against the world; everything moved around Guido as its center. It still does, but while it does, it makes music. I laugh at this, waiting at the top of the slope for a gap in the traffic; always careful, I will not be seen dropping over the rail to the embankment below. I—

—hear a note and all sound, all singing stops for a moment; sight too, I think, and touch; a wave, a wrench, a great peace, and then I am back on the high road, holding the rail, clamping my violin case under my coat, looking at the sky. I am different. The . . . meaning of "I" is different. . . .

All across the city, like distant thunder heard in a high wind, there is a whisper of breaking metal, a twinkling of explosion and fire, and no music. To none of this do I pay attention; I am watching that which is slipping down out of the sky. A silver ball, and under it, four machines like tanks, their four long necks twined together, their four heads stacked neatly one on the other. But for the deep hooting which comes from these heads, they fall silently.

I take off my trench coat and let it fall. I open the violin case, take out the violin, strike the railing once with it, pull out the four pegs, clear away the strings with two quick swipes, until I hold only the smooth neck and fingerboard, which ends in the widening curled scroll.

I run downhill as fast as I can, faster than I have ever run before. I know I shall be met, by whom, how, and exactly when. It is an old Hispano-Suiza with wide flaring fenders and big yellow headlights, driven by a woman. I see the car coming, run straight down the middle of the road. She slows but does not stop. I leap to the front of the car, turn, hook a knee over the headlight brace, grasp the radiator ornament. She is already howling up the hill; faster she goes, and faster, all that mighty automobile can put out.

Acceleration pressure lessens and frees me; I move myself, get one foot on the hood and the other on the radiator, still holding with one hand to the headlight brace. It has all happened quickly; I have been riding perhaps twenty, twenty-five seconds. We are back to the top of the slope and traveling eighty, ninety kilometers . . . who has made these observations and calculations as to our speed, the slope, the rate of descent of the globe and its machines, how close they must pass the rail? No matter who . . . it has been done, and every slightest pull of her wrists, each lean and striving of my body against the wind, is part of those calculations; I know it, know it is right, without wonder and without astonishment . . . for I have calculated it all; I know how; it must be right, I know so very well how. (And "I" means something new now.)

She turns to the left and the front wheels shudder over the curb. I let go the brace and put my feet side by side on the radiator, and as the front of the car reaches the railing I spring up and out, flying as men have in their hearts always wished to fly . . . up and up into the dark. With my ears I know my speed, air rushing past, diminishing as I reach the top of my arc and begin to descend; it is in this poised moment that I meet the machines from the sky, with my left arm and both legs taking those intertwined metal necks. Below me the Hispano is turning end over end down the embankment.

I reach up with my violin neck, holding it by the flat protruding lower end of the ebony fingerboard, and find that with the other end, the hard curved polished scroll, I can reach the open trumpet mouth of the topmost head. It accepts the slight curve of the carving exactly; I ram it home, extract it, repeat the motion on the second, third, fourth, crushing some delicate something in the joined throats of each.

Then that pervasive hooting is gone, and we drift silently for a second—but only a second; we are on the ground near and between two of the stilts which support the road. A sort of curtain hangs there; as we touch earth, this curtain topples outward and falls across the globe. There are people—three women, four men. One of the men is old, and wears nothing but a wooden leg strapped to his thigh. One of the women wears an ermine jacket; the tall heels are broken off her shoes. They seize a rope and run, and drop a steel hook into the girders of the stilt. On the other side, a girl and a man, an impossibly fat man, place a hook on the other side. The hard fabric of the curtain smashes at me as I struggle free—it is one of those enormous woven mats of steel-cored hempen cable they use to cover rocks when dynamiting in the city. They have captured the globe with it, casting it like a net over birds! And the globe fights; it fights, plunging upward, making no sound. The net holds, the ropes hold; I hear the steel hooks crackle in the girders as they slip and grab. The plunging stops; the globe presses upward, trying and trying to break free. The anchor ropes hum, the net rustles with strain. I feel a warmth, a heat, from the globe; it drops abruptly, plunges upward once more, but weakly, and suddenly falls to the ground with the rope mat shrouding it and smoking. The four tanklike machines have not moved since they landed; with their voices gone they have no function.

The woman in ermine and the fat man run to a two-wheeled dolly standing under the roadway. I run to help them. Nobody speaks. It is an acetylene set. We drag it to the dead sphere and light it. We begin to cut the sphere open so that I—this new, wide, deep, all-over-the-world "I"—can see what it is, how it works.

I—and "I," now, think as I work of what is happening —a different kind of thinking than any I have ever known . . . if thinking was seeing, then all my life I have thought in a hole in the ground, and now I think on a mountaintop. To think of any question is to think of the answer, if the answer exists in the experience of any other part of "I." If I wonder why I was chosen to make that leap from the car, using all my strength and all its speed to carry me exactly to that point in space where the descending machines would be, then the wonder doesn't last long enough to be called that: I *know* why I was chosen, on the instant of wondering. Someone had measured the throat of one of the tank machines; someone knew what tool would fit it exactly and be right to destroy it most easily. The neck and scroll of my violin happened to be that tool, and I happened to be on the high road with it. I might have died. The woman driving the Hispano did die. These are things that do not matter; one will unhesitatingly break a fingernail in reaching to snatch a child from the fire.

Yet, as all knowledge of the greater "I" is available to me, so is all feeling. The loss of my violin before I had made the first single note with it is a hurt beyond bearing; its loss in so important an action does not diminish the hurt at all. But to think of the hurt is to know all hurts, everywhere, of all of us who are now so strangely joined. Now there was a little boy in America, who when it was time threw himself into the drive of one of the tank machines because "I" required that the drive slip just so much, just at that second. It is known to me now that the child Henry wanted hungrily to live, more than ever in his little life before, because he had, within the hour, experienced a half second of real peace. It hurt him, dying; knowing him as I (as "I") do, it hurts to have him dead. Near him died a man, Paul, unhesitatingly, feeling the most pointed loss of a woman he desired to the moment he died, and whom he had almost possessed a moment before. There are many such deaths at this moment, all over the world, and not one which "I" cannot feel; all are known to me—the helpless, so many of whom lie this minute crushed in their cars and houses, who crawl numbly away from the fires, not fast enough to get away. These are dying too, and hurting, and even these know Guido and Guido's loss; *Unfair, unfair,* they cry as they bleed and die; *you should not have lost your violin so soon!* All, all add themselves to me; all, all understand. I belong, belong; I, Guido, belong!

We have struck back with whatever would do the job, wherever it could be found, regardless of the cost, because no cost is too great to combat what has come upon us.

We will take care of our own; "I" will defend "myself." And meanwhile the pressure of Guido's music floods "me" and enriches the species, and Guido is enriched in numberless ways to an infinite degree. This is thinking as never before; this is living as never before; this is a life to be defended to a degree and in ways never before realized on this earth. . . . I wonder if anyone will ever speak again?

# CHAPTER 24

Sharon Brevix thought, *I can see all over the world.*
And she thought, *They've found me.*

You're four and you're lost: what bothers you?
Hunger, cold, but mostly disorientation—detachment:
not knowing where to go or where "they" all are.
Sharon awoke where she had dozed off . . . rather, where
she had slipped so very far over the slippery edge of the
forever-dark. It was slippery no longer. She was hungry,
she was cold, certainly; but *she wasn't lost.*

Suppose her mother were here—what would she do?
*Are you all right?* Well, she was all right. Nothing
broken, no cuts; no encounters with the bestial in any
form. Her mother knew that and Sharon knew she
knew that. The closeness she felt to her mother and to
Billy and the other kids wasn't quite as nice as having
them here, and being warm and having something to
eat. But there were new ways, other ways, that were
nicer—nicer than anything she had ever known. Billy
now—see how glad he was, how afraid he'd been. How
much he cared. It made her feel very good to know that
Billy cared so much. It had always been his best-kept
secret.

She knew she must sleep for an hour, so she closed her

eyes and slept. It was quite a different thing from that other sleep.

When she awoke for the second time, it was instantly and with instant motion. She bounced to her feet no matter how stiff she felt and marked time, double-time, on a flat rock, banging her feet until they stung, and breathing deeply. Three minutes of that and she struck off purposefully into the still-dark underbrush, skipped on two stepping-stones across the brook, and unhesitatingly went to a fallen log where, the night before, she had seen a bright orange shelf fungus. She broke off large greedy pieces and crammed her mouth full of them. It was delicious, and safe, too, because although most people did not know it, someone, somewhere did know that this particular pileus was edible.

She trotted back to the half-cave where she had spent the night and got Mary Lou, her broken-footed doll, and fed her some of the fungus and a few drops of water from the brook. Then, cautioning the doll not to say a word, she set off through the woods.

In less than an hour, and while the light was still gray, she found herself at the edge of a meadow. She raised a warning finger at Mary Lou, and then stood still as a tree-trunk—an unnatural act for any child before now—and peered through the dawn-light until she saw a rabbit. It was aware of her and fear-frozen into exactly her immobility. Sharon outwaited it, let it move, let it move again, let it nibble on young clover and stare at her again and at last move curiously closer. When it was close enough, she pounced, not at the rabbit but at the place where the rabbit would be when she moved. The rabbit was there.

She transferred her grasp on the dew-damp, kicking

creature to a one-handed grip just over the joints of the hind legs and stood up, lifting the rabbit clear of the ground. As it hung upside down, it immediately swung its head up and forward (as someone, somewhere, knew it would). Sharon brought the edge of her left hand down with a single smart chop, and broke its neck. She squatted down, and unhesitatingly nibbled a hole in the animal's throat with her sharp front teeth. She drank as much blood as she needed, offered some to Mary Lou (who didn't want any) wiped her mouth daintily with a handful of moist grass, picked up her doll and went her purposeful way. She knew which way to go. She knew where the road was and where a railroad was and where three farmhouses and a hunting lodge were. She also knew which one to go to, and that Daddy would come to pick her up, and that she would be at the meeting place before Daddy would, and which cellar window she was allowed to break to get in, and where the can opener was and how to prime the pump to get water. It was pretty wonderful. All she had to do was to need to know something, and if anyone knew it, she knew it.

She walked along happily, for a while sharing a stomach-shrinking thrill with some child, somewhere, who was riding a roller-coaster, and for a while doing a new kind of talking with her father. It was a tease; he'd have said to her, before: "I thought you were in the station wagon and Mummy thought you were in the truck. Good thing we were wrong. There'd've been two of you, and then who'd wear the pink dress?" But now it came out as a kind of picture, or maybe a memory of two Sharons screeching at each other and pulling at the party dress, while two broken-footed Mary Lous looked

134

on. It was funny and she laughed. It was more than a memory. It was all the relieved anxiety and deep fondness and self-accusation her Daddy felt over almost losing his Princess-Wicked-wif'-the-fickles-on-her-nose.

She reached the lodge and got in all right. After about an hour she looked out the window and saw a bush rattlesnake in the bare patch by the shed. She ran to the gun-cabinet and then to the bookcase for the box of .32 cartridges, and loaded the revolver and put it down and got the window open a crack and picked up the gun and braced it against the sill and got it lined up until she, or somebody, knew it was just right. Then she squeezed off a single shot that eliminated the snake's head. She unloaded the gun and ran a swab through it and put it away, and put the shells away, and then built a play-house out of overturned furniture and sofa cushions, in which she and Mary Lou fell fast asleep until Tony Brevix got there. All in all, she had a wonderful time. She never once had to wonder whether she was allowed to do this or that—she *knew*. Most important, she was by herself and in a new place, but she wasn't lost. She would never be lost again. If only nothing spoiled this, no one in the world would ever be lost again, no, nor wonder if somebody really loved them, or think they'd gone away and left them because they didn't want them.

It had always been thus between Sharon and Mary Lou, because Mary Lou knew Sharon loved her even when she accidentally left her out in the rain or threw her down the stairs. Now the children understood that kind of thing as well as the dolls, and never again would a child wonder if anyone cared, or grow up thinking that to be loved is a privilege. It's a privilege only to adults. To any child it's a basic right, which if denied dooms the child to a lifetime of seeking it and an inability to accept anything but child-style love. The way things were now, never again would a child be afraid of growing up, or hover anxiously near half-empty coffers so very easy to fill.

*I know your need,* the whole world was saying to "I," while "I" everywhere could understand the justice of "my" needs, and the silliness of so many wants.

When Tony Brevix came into the lodge he found her asleep. He knew she was aware of him and he knew that her awareness would not interrupt her slumber, not for a second. She slept smiling while he carried her out to the station wagon.

# CHAPTER 25

*There she stands the water beading her bright body her head to one side the water sparking off her hair, she smiles, says All Right Handsome What Are You Going To Do About It?*

Crash!

A soft rumble and a glare of light: sky. Crash! A brighter, unbearable flash of light on light, a sharp smell of burning chemicals, a choking cloud of dust and smoke and the patter-patter of falling debris. Confusion, bewilderment, disorientation and growing anger at the deprivation of a dream.

The sharp command to every sentience, mechanical or not, on the entire hilltop: *Get Gurlick out of here!*

A flash of silver overhead, then a strange overall sticky, pore-choking sensation, like being coated with warm oil, and underneath, the torn hill dwindles away. There are still hundreds of projectors left, row on row of them, but from the size of the terraces where they are parked, there must have been hundreds of thousands more. *Crash!* A half dozen of the projectors bulge skyward and fall back in shatters and shards. Look there, a flight of jets. See, two silver spheres, dodging, dancing: then the long curve of a seeking missile points one out,

137

and the trail and the burst make a bright ball on a smoky string, painted across the sky. *Crash! Crash!* Even as the scarred hill disappears in swift distance, the parked projectors can be seen bursting skyward, a dozen and a dozen and a score of them, pressing upward through the rain of pieces from those blasted a breath or a blink ago; and *cra—*

No, not *crash* this time, but a point, a porthole, a bay-window looking in to the core of hell, all the colors and all too bright, growing, too, too big to be growing so fast, taking the hilltop, the hillside, the whole hill lost in the ball of brilliance.

And for minutes afterward, hanging stickily by something invisible, frighteningly in midair under the silver sphere, but not feeling wind or acceleration or any of the impossible turns as the sphere whizzes along low, hedge-hopping, ground-hugging, back-tracking and hovering to hide; for minutes and minutes afterward, through the drifting speckles of overdazzled eyeballs, the pastel column can be seen rising and rising flat-headed over the land, thousands and thousands of feet, building a roof with eaves, the eaves curling and curling out and down, or are they the grasping fingers of rows and rows of what devils who have climbed up the inside of the spout, about to put up *what* hellish faces?

"Bastits," Gurlick whimpered, "tryin' to atom-bomb *me*. You tell 'em who I am?"

No response. The Medusa was calculating, for once, to capacity—even to its immense, infinitely varied capacity. It had expected to succeed in unifying the mind of humanity—it had correctly predicted its certainty of success and the impossibility of failure. But success like *this?*

Like this: In the first forty minutes humanity destroyed seventy-one per cent of the projectors and forty-three percent of the spheres. To do this it used everything and anything that came to hand, regardless of the cost in lives or matériel; it put out its fire by smothering it with its mink coat. It killed its cobra by hitting it with the baby. It moved, reactive and accurate and almost in reflex, like a man holding a burning stick, and as the heat increases near one finger, it will release and withdraw and find another purchase while he thinks of other things. It threw a child into the drive of a projector because he fit, he contained the right amount of the right grade of lubricant for just that purpose at just that time. It could understand in microseconds that the nearest thing to the exact necessary tool for tearing the throat out of a projector would be the neck and scroll of a violin.

And like this: Beginning in the forty-first minute, humanity launched the first precision weapon against the projectors, having devised and produced a seeking mechanism which would infallibly find and destroy projectors (though they did not radiate in the electromagnetic spectrum, not even infra-red) and then made it compact enough to cram into the warhead of a Hawk, and, further, applied the Hawk to the Atlas. And this was only the first. In the fifty-second minute—that is, less than an hour after the Medusa pushed the button to unify the mind of man—humanity was using hasty makeshifts of appalling efficiency, devices which reversed the steering commands of the projectors (like the one which under its own power walked off the Hell Gate Bridge into eighty feet of water) and others which rebroadcast the projectors' signals 180 degrees out of phase, nullifying them. At the ninety-minute mark humanity was knocking out two of every three flying spheres it saw, not by accurate aiming (because as yet humanity couldn't tool up to countermeasure inertia-less turns at six miles per second) but by an ingenious application of the theory of random numbers, by which they placed proximity missiles where the sphere wasn't but almost certainly would be—and all too often was.

The Medusa had anticipated success. But, to sum up: success like *this*? For hadn't the humans stamped out every operable instrument of the Medusa's invasion (save Gurlick, about whom they couldn't know) in just two hours and eight minutes?

This incredible species, uniquely possessed of a defense against the Medusa (the Medusa still stubbornly insisted) in its instant, total fragmentation at the invader's first touch, seemed uniquely to possess other qualities as well. It would be wise—more: it was imperative—that Earth be brought into the fold where it would have to take orders. Hence— Gurlick.

It swept Gurlick back into its confidence, told him that in spite of the abruptness of his awakening, he was now ready to go out on his own. It described to him his assignment, which made Gurlick snicker like an eight-year-old behind the barn, and assured him that it would set up for him the most perfect opportunity its mighty computers could devise. Speed, however, was of the essence—which was all right with Gurlick, who spit on his hands and made cluck-cluck noises from his back teeth and wrinkled up half his face with an obscene wink, and snickered again to show his willingness.

The sphere hovered now at treetop level over heavily wooded ground, keeping out of sight while awaiting the alien computation of the best conceivable circumstances for Gurlick's project. This might well have proved lengthy, based as it was on Gurlick's partial, mistaken, romantic, deluded and downright pornographic information, and might even have supplied some highly amusing conclusions, since they would have been based on logic, and Gurlick's most certainly were not. These diverting computations were lost, however, and lost forever when the sphere dropped dizzyingly, released Gurlick so abruptly that he tumbled, and informed him that he was on his own—the sphere was detected. Growling and grumbling, Gurlick sprawled under the trees and watched the sphere bullet upward and away, and a moment later the appearance of a Hawk, or rather its trail, scoring the sky in a swift reach like the spread of a strain-crack in window glass.

He did not see the inevitable, but heard it in due course—the faint distant thump against the roof of the world which marked the end of the sphere's existence—and very probably the end of all the Medusa's artifacts on earth. He said an unprintable syllable, rolled over and eyed the woodlands with disfavor. This wasn't going to be like flying over it like a bug over a carpet, with some big brain doing all your thinking for you. On the other hand . . . this was the payoff. This was where Gurlick got his—where at long last he could strike back at a whole world full of bastits.

He got to his feet and began walking.

# CHAPTER 26

Full of wonder, the human hive contemplated itself and its works, its gains, its losses and its new nature.

First, there was the intercommunication—a thing so huge, so different, that few minds could previously have imagined it. No analogy could suffice; no concepts of infinite telephone exchanges, or multi-side-band receivers, could hint at the quality of that gigantic cognizance. To describe it in terms of its complexity would be as impossible—and as purblind—as an attempt to describe fine lace by a description of each of its threads. It had, rather, *texture*. Your memory, and his and his, and hers over the horizon's shoulder—all your memories are mine. More: your personal orientation in the framework of your own experiences, your I-in-the-past, is also mine. More: your skills remain your own (is great music made less for being shared?) but your sensitivity to your special subject is mine now, and your pride in your excellence is mine now. More: though bound to the organism, Mankind, as never before, I am I as never before. When Man has demands on me, I am totally dedicated to Man's purpose. Otherwise, within the wide, wide limits of mankind's best interests, I am as never before a free agent; I am I to a greater degree, and with less obstruction from within and without, than ever before possible. For gone, gone altogether are individual man's hosts of pests and devils, which in strange combinations have plagued us all in the past: the They-don't-want-me devil, the Suppose-they-find-out devil, the twin imps of They-are-lying-to-me and They-are-trying-to-cheat-me; gone, gone is I'm-afraid-to-try, and They-won't-let-me, and I-couldn't-be-loved-if-they-knew.

Along with the imps and devils, other things disappeared—things regarded throughout human history as basic, thematic, keys to the structures of lives and cultures. Now if a real thing should disappear, a rock or a tree or a handful of water, there will be thunder and a wind and other violence, depending upon what form the vanished mass owned. Or if a great man disappears, there is almighty confusion in the rush to fill the vacuum of his functions. But the things which disappeared now proved their unreality by the unruffled silence in which they disappeared. Money. The sense of property. Jingoistic patriotism, tariffs, taxes, boundaries and frontiers, profit and loss, hatred and suspicion of humans by humans, and language itself (except as part of an art) with all the difficulties of communication between languages and within them.

In short, it was abruptly possible for mankind to live with itself in health. Removed now was mankind's cess-gland, the secretions of which (called everything from cussedness to Original Sin) had poisoned its body since it was born, distorting decencies like survival and love into greed and lust, turning Achievement ("I have built") into Position ("I have power").

So much for humanity's new state of being. As to its

143

abilities, they were simply based, straightforward. There are always many ways to accomplish anything, but only one of them is really best. Which of them is best—that is the source of all argument on the production of anything, the creator of factions among the designers, and the first enemy of speed and efficiency. But when humanity became a hive, and needed something—as for example the adaptation of the swift hunting missile Hawk to the giant carrier Atlas—the device was produced without considerations of pride or profit, without waste motion, and without interpersonal friction of any kind. The decision was made, the job was done. In those heady first moments, anything and everything available was used—but with precision. Later (by minutes) fewer ingenious stopgaps were used, more perfect tools were shaped from the materials at hand. And still later (by hours) there was full production of new designs. Mankind now used exactly the right tool for the jobs it had to do. . . .

And within it, each individual flowered, finding freedoms to be, to act, to take enrichment and pleasure as never before. What were the things that Dimity (Salomé?) Carmichael had always needed, wanted to do? She could do them now. An Italian boy, Guido, packed taut with talent, awaited the arrival of the greatest living violinist from behind a now collapsed Iron Curtain; they would hereafter spend their lives and do their work together. The parents of a small stiff boy named Henry contemplated, as all the world contemplated, what had happened to him and why, and how totally impossible it would be for such a thing ever to happen again. Sacrifice there must be from time to time, even now; but never again a useless one. Everyone now

144

knew, as if in personal memory, how fiercely Henry had wanted to live in that flash of agony which had eclipsed him. All Earth shared the two kinds of religious experience discovered by the Africans Mbala and Nuyu, wherein one had become confirmed in his faith and the other had found it. What, specifically, had brought them to it was of no significance; the fact of their devotion was the important thing to be shared, for it is in the finest nature of humanity to worship, fight it as he sometimes may. The universe being what it is, there is always *plus ultra, plus ultra*—powers and patterns beyond understanding, and more beyond these when these are understood. Out there is the call to which faith is the natural response and worship the natural approach.

Such was humanity when it became a hive—a beautiful entity, balanced and fine and wondrously alive. A pity, in a way, that such a work of art, such self-sufficiency, was to exist in this form for so brief a time. . . .

# CHAPTER 27

Gurlick, alone of humans insulated from the human hive, member of another, sensed none of this. Driven, hungry through a whole spectrum of appetites, full of resentment, he shuffled through the woods. He had been vaguely aware of the outskirts of a town not far from where the silver sphere had set him down; he would, he supposed, find what he wanted there, though wanting it was the only thing quite clear to him. How he was to get it was uncertain; but get it he must. He was aware of the presence within him of the Medusa, observing, computing, but—not directing, cognizant as it was of the fact that the fine details of such an operation must be left to the species itself. Had it had its spheres and other machines available, there might have been a great deal it could do to assist Gurlick. But now—he was on his own.

He was in virgin forest now, the interlocked foliage overhead dimming the mid-morning sunshine to an underwater green, and the footing was good, there being little underbrush and a gentle downslope. Gurlick gravitated downhill, knowing he would encounter a path or a road sooner or later, and monotonously cursed his empty stomach, his aching feet, and his enemies.

He heard voices.

He stopped, shrank back against a tree trunk, and peered. For a moment he could detect nothing, and then, off to the right, he heard a sudden musical laugh. He looked toward the sound, and saw a brief motion of something blue. He came out of hiding, and, scuttling clumsily from tree to tree, went to investigate.

There were three of them, girls in their mid-teens, dressed in halters and shorts, giggling over the chore of building a fire in a small clearing. They had a string of fish, pike and lake trout, and a frying pan, and seemed completely and hilariously preoccupied.

Gurlick, from a vantage point above them, chewed on his lower lip and wondered what to do. He had no delusions about approaching openly and sweet-talking his way into their circle. It would be far wiser, he knew, to slip away and go looking elsewhere, for something surer, safer. On the other hand . . . he heard the crackle of bacon fat as one of the girls dropped the tender slivers into the frying pan. He looked at the three lithe young bodies, and at the waiting string of fish, half of which were scaled and beheaded, and quietly moaned. There was too much of what was wanted, down there, for him to turn his back.

Then a curl of fragrance from the bacon reached him and toppled his reason. He rose from his crouch and in three bounds was down the slope and in their midst, moaning and slavering. One of the children bounded away to the right, one to the left. The third fell under his hands, shrieking.

"Now you jus' be still," he panted, trying to hold his victim, trying to protect himself against her hysterical slappings, writhings, clawings. "I ain't goin' to hurt you if you jus'—"

*Uh!* He was bowled right off his feet by one of the escapees who had returned at a dead run and crashed him with a hard shoulder. He rolled over and found himself staring up at the second girl who had run away as she stood over him with a stone the size of a grape-fruit raised in both hands. She brought it down; it hit Gurlick on the left cheekbone and the bridge of his nose and filled the world with stars and brilliant tatters of pain. He fell back, wagging his head, pawing at his face, trying to get some vision back and kick away the sick dizziness; and when at last he could see again, he was alone with the campfire, the frying pan, the string of fish.

"Li'l bastits," he growled, holding his face. He looked at his hand, on which were flecks of his own blood, swore luridly, turned in a circle as if to find and pursue them, and then squatted before the fire, reached for two cleaned fish, and dropped them hissing into the pan.

Well, he'd get that much out of it, anyway.

He had eaten four of the fish and had two more cooking when he heard voices again, a man's deep, "Which way now? Over here?" and a girl's answer, "Yes, where the smoke's coming from."

Jailbait . . . of course, of *course* they'd have gone for help! Gurlick cursed them all and lumbered down-slope, away from the sound of voices. Boy, he'd messed up, but good. The whole hillside would be crawling with people hunting him. He had to get out of here.

He moved as cautiously as he could, quite sure he was being watched by hundreds of eyes, yet seeing no one until he glimpsed two men off to his left and below him. One had binoculars on a strap around his neck, the other a shotgun. Gurlick, half-fainting with terror, slumped down between a tree trunk and a rock, and cowered there until he could hear their voices, and while he heard them, and after he heard them, with their curt certain syllables and their cold lack of mercy. When all was quite quiet again, he rose, and at that moment became aware of an aircraft sound. It approached rapidly, and he dropped back into his hiding place, trembling, and peeped up at the glittering patches of blue in the leafy roof. The machine flew directly overhead, low, too slowly—a helicopter. He heard it thrashing the air off to the north, downhill from him, and for a while he could not judge if it was going or coming or simply circling down there. In his pride he was convinced that its business was Gurlick and only Gurlick, and in his ignorance he was certain it had seen him through the thick cover. It went away at last, and the forest returned to its murmuring silence. He heard a faint shout behind and above him, and scuttled from cover and away from the sound. Pausing, a moment later, for breath, he caught another glimpse of the man with the shotgun off to his left, and escaped to the right and down.

And, thus pursued and herded, he came to the water's edge.

There was a dirt path there, and no one in sight; and it was warm and sunny and peaceful. Slowly Gurlick's panic subsided, and, as he walked along the path, there was a deep throb of anticipation within him. He'd gotten away clean; he had outdistanced his enemies and now, enemies, beware!

The path curved closer to the bank of the lake. Alders

149

stood thick here, and there was the smell of moss. The path turned, and the shade was briefly darker here at the verge of the floods of gold over the water. And there by the path it lay, the little pile of fabric, bright red, shiny black, filmy white with edges iced with lace. . . .

Gurlick stopped walking, stopped breathing until his chest hurt. Then he moved slowly past this incredible, impossible consolidation of his dream, and went to the bushes at the water's edge.

She was out there—*she*.

He made a sharp wordless sound and stood forward, away from the bushes. She turned in the water and stared at him, her eyes round.

Emancipated now, free to be what she had always wished to be, and to do what she needed to do without fear or hesitation; swimming now naked in the sun, sure and fearless, shameless; utterly oriented within herself and herself within the matrix of humanity and all its known data, Salomé Carmichael stood up in the water, under the sun, and said, "Hello, Handsome."

# CHAPTER 28

So ended humanity within its planetary limits; so ended the self-contained, self-aware species-hive which had for such a brief time been able to feel, to the ends of its earth, its multifarious self. The end came some hours after the helicopter—the same one which had set her down by the pond—had come for Salomé Carmichael, which it had the instant Gurlick quit the scene. Gurlick had seen it from where he crouched guiltily in the bushes. After it had gone away he slowly climbed to his feet and made his way back to the pond. He hunkered down with his back to a tree and regarded the scene unwinkingly.

It had been right there, on the moss.

Over there had lain the pretty little heap of clothes, so clean, so soft, so very red, shiny black, the white so pretty. The strangest thing that had ever happened to him in his whole life had happened here, stranger than the coming of the Medusa, stranger than the unpeopled factory back there in the mountains, stranger, even, than the overwhelming fact of this place, of her being here, of the unbelievable coincidence of it all with his dream. And that strangest thing of all was that once, when she was here, she had cried out, and he had then been gentle. He had been gentle with all his heart and mind and body, for a brief while flooded, melted, swept away by gentleness. No wrinkled raisin from out of space, no concept like the existence of a single living thing so large it permeated two galaxies and part of a third, could be so shockingly alien to him, everything he was and had ever been, as this rush of gentleness. Its microscopic seed must have lain encysted within him all his life, never encountering a single thing, large or small, which could warm it to germination. Now it had burst open, burst him open, and he was shocked, shaken, macerated as never before in his bruised existence.

He crouched against the tree and regarded the moss, and the lake, and the place where the red and the black and the lace had lain, and wondered why he had run away. He wondered how he could have let her go. The gentleness was consuming him, even now . . . he had to find somewhere to put it down, but there wouldn't be anyone else, anyone or anything, for him to be gentle to, anywhere in the world.

He began to cry. Gurlick had always wept easily, his facile tears his only outlet for fear, and anger, and humiliation, and spite. This, however, was different. This was very difficult to do, painful in the extreme, and impossible to stop until he was racked, wrung out, exhausted. It tumbled him over and left him groveling on the moss. Then he slept, abruptly, his whipped consciousness fleeing away to the dark.

# CHAPTER 29

What can travel faster than light?

Stand here by me, friend, on this hillside, under the black and freckled sky. Which stars do you know—Polaris? Good. And the bright one yonder, that's Sirius. Look at them now: at Polaris, at Sirius. Quickly now: Polaris, Sirius. And again: Sirius, Polaris.

How far apart are they? It says in the book, thousands of light-years. How many? Too many: never mind. But how long does it take you to flick your gaze from one to the other and back? a second? A half-second next time, then a tenth? . . . You can't say that nothing, absolutely nothing, has traveled between the two. Your vision has; your attention has.

You now understand, you have the rudiments of understanding what it is to flick a part of yourself from star to star, just as (given the skill) you may shift from soul to soul.

With such a shift, down such a path, came the Medusa at the instant of its marriage to humanity. In all the history of humanity, the one instant (save death) of most significance is the instant of syngamy, the moment of penetration by the sperm of the ovum. Yet almost never is there a heralding of this instant, nor a sign; it comes to pass in silence and darkness, and no one ever knows but the mindless flecks of complex jelly directly involved.

Not so now; and never before, and never again would marriage occur with such explosion. A microsecond after that melding, Gurlick's altered seed to the welcoming ovum of a human, the Medusa of space shot down its contacting thread, an unerring harpoon carrying a line to itself, and all of its Self following in the line, ready to reach and fill humanity, make of it a pseudopod, the newest member of its sprawling corpus.

But if the Medusa's bolt can be likened to a harpoon, then it can be said that the uprushing flood it met was like a volcano. The Medusa had not a micro-microsecond in which to realize what had happened to it. It did not die; it was not killed any more than humanity would have been killed had the Medusa's plan been realized. Humanity would have become a "person" of the illimitable creature. Now . . .

Now, instead, humanity became the creature; flooded it, filled it to its furthermost crannies, drenched its most remote cells with the Self of humankind. Die? Never that; the Medusa was alive as never before, with a new and different kind of life, in which its slaves were freed but its motivations unified; where the individual was courted and honored and brought special nutrients, body and mind, and where, freely, "want to" forever replaced "must."

And all for want of a datum: that intelligence might exist in individuals, and that dissociated individuals might co-operate and yet not be a hive. For there is no structure on earth which could not have been built by rats, were the rats centrally directed and properly motivated. How could the Medusa have known? Thousands upon thousands of species and cultures throughout the galaxies have technological progress as advanced as that of Earth, and are yet composed of individuals no more highly evolved than termites, lemurs, or shrews. What slightest hint was there for the Medusa that a hive-humanity would be a different thing from a super-rat?

Humanity had passed the barriers of language and of individual isolation on its planet. It passed the barriers of species now, and of isolation in its cosmos. The faith of Mbala was available to Guido, and so were the crystal symphonies of the black planets past Ophiuchus. Charlotte Dunsay, reaching across the world to her husband in Hobart, Tasmania, might share with him a triple sunrise in the hub of Orion's great Nebula. As one man could share the *being* of another here on earth, so both, and perhaps a small child with them, could fuse their inner selves with some ancient contemplative mind leeched to the rocks in some roaring methane cataract, or soar with some insubstantial life-forms adrift where they were born in the high layers of atmosphere around some unheard-of planet.

So ended mankind, to be born again as hive-humanity; so ended the hive of earth to become star-man, the immeasurable, the limitless, the growing; maker of music beyond music, poetry beyond words, and full of wonder, full of worship.

# CHAPTER 30

So too ended Gurlick, the isolated, alone among human-kind denied membership in the fusion of humans, full of a steaming fog, aglow with his flickerings of hate and the soft shine of corruption, member of something other than humankind. For while humanity had been able to read him (and his dream) and herd him through the forest to its fulfillment, it had never been able to reach his consciousness, blocked as it was by the thought-lines of the Medusa.

These lines, however, were open still, and when humanity became Medusa, it flooded down to Gurlick and made him welcome. *Come!* it called, and whirled him up and outward, showing and sharing its joy and strength and pride, showering him with wonders of a thousand elsewheres and a hundred heres; it showed him how to laugh at the most rarefied technician's joke and how to feel the structure of sestinae and sonnets, of bridges and Bach. It spoke to him saying *We* and grant-ing him the right to regard it all and say: *I*. And more: he had been promised a kingship, and now he had it, for all this sentient immensity acknowledged to him its debt. Let him but make the phantom of a wish of a thought, and his desires would be fulfilled. *Come!* it called. *Come!*

But the weight of the man o' war was on his mind. *Hide!* he thought. Don't attract attention. If he got out of line, the man o' war would squash him like a bug. But humanity, which had become Medusa, insisted, it beat down upon him, and finally Gurlick could withstand its force no longer. He turned and faced humankind as it had become, all-transcending, all-inclusive, all-knowing, pervasive—faced humankind as he had never faced it before in his life.

Humankind had changed.

His first reaction was *My God, it's full of people!*

Which was strange, because he found himself at the edge of a purple cliff which overlooked a valley with a silver river in it. Not silver like the poets say, which only means the reflection of sky-white; this one was metallic silver color, fluid, fast. He was aware without surprise that he sat on the tip of his spine, which was long, black and tapering, with two enormous hind legs, kneed in the middle like broken straws and pretty nearly as slender, forming the other two points of his tripod. He was chewing on a stone, holding it to black marble lips (which opened sidewise) with four hands (having scorpion-nippers for fingers) and he found it delicious. He turned his head around (all the way, without effort) and saw Salomé Carmichael behind him, and she was beautiful beyond belief, which was odd because she looked like a twelve-foot, blue-black praying mantis. But then, so did he.

She spoke, but it was not speech really, but a sort of semaphore of the emotions. He felt himself greeted, and made joyfully welcome *(Hello, oh hello, Danny, I knew you'd come, you had to come)* and then there was an invitation: *to the place to watch that game.* She moved close to him so that their bodies touched, and somehow he knew just exactly what to do to stay with her; in a blink they were somewhere else, on the top of a swaying green tree (the bark was the green part) and he had a round blunt front end like a bull-frog and four gauzy wings, and two long legs with webbed feet like a waterbird. Salomé was there too, of the same species and utterly lovely; and together they watched the game, understanding it as completely in all its suspensions and convolutions as any Earthside hockey or baseball or chess fan might follow his favorite. The teams were whole hives, and they could, all together, create soundwaves and focus them; at the focal point danced a bluegreen crystal, held spinning in midair by the beam of sound. There were three hive-teams, not two, and if two should focus together on the crystal it would shatter musically, and that was a foul, and the third team won the point, and could have the playing field to dance in. And when the dance was over (there were points for the dance too) then another crystal would be projected high in the rosy air. . . .

To a swimming place, tingling, refreshing, Gurlick knowing somehow that where they swam under a blueblack rock ceiling, the temperature was over a thousand degrees centigrade, and the gleaming bony paddles and sleek speckled flanks with which he swam and on which he felt the tingling were no flesh he had ever learned of. And to a flying place where all the people, welcoming as everywhere, and some known to him as people he had met on Earth, all these people were cobweb-frail, spending their lives adrift in the thin shifts of air with the highest mist peaks of a cloud-shrouded planet as their floor. . . .

And Salomé gave him her story of envy and of her need to have others depend on her.

These two were ideal antagonists, ideal weapons in the conflict between Medusa and mankind. Medusa had won the battles; mankind had won the war. And it had all begun with Gurlick. . . .

Somewhere in this communion between them, the whole thing was talked out. It was probably in the first couple of seconds of their first meeting, there over the silver river. If it were rendered into words it was Gurlick's complete wounding by the discovery (in his loneliness) that what had happened by the lake was no affair of his at all, but only a strategic move in a war between a giant and a behemoth; with it, all he had ever been in his tattered life, how there was nothing within him with a whole soul to give in exchange for accidental kindness; how he was unashamed to have far, far passed the point where he could keep clean and think well and be a man . . . in short, the entire Gurlick, with all the reasons why, in one clear flash.

Gurlick, numb and passive as he tossed like a chip on their ocean of wonders, had at last a wish, and had it, and had it.

True, none of this could have come about without him. This result could not have been with anyone else in his place, so—true enough—he was owed a debt. Pay it, then.

Pay the debt. . . . You do not reward a catalyst by changing it, the unchanging, into something else. When a man is what Gurlick is, he is that because he has made himself so; for what his environment has done to him, blame the environment not so much as the stolid will that kept him in it. So—take away hunger and poverty (of body and soul), deprivation and discomfort and humiliation, and you take away the very core of his being—his sole claim to superiority.

You take away his hate. You take away from him all reason to hate anyone or anything—like the wet, like the cold.

So don't ask him to look out among the stars, and join in the revelries of giants. Don't thank him, don't treat him, and above all, do not so emasculate him as to take away from him his reasons to hate: they have become his life.

So they paid him, meticulously to the specifications he himself (though all unknowing) set up.

And as long as he lived, there was a city-corner, drab streets and fumes, sullen pedestrians and careless, dangerous aimers of trucks and cabs; moist unbearable heat and bitter cold; and bars where Gurlick could go and put in his head, whining for a drink, and bartenders to send him out into the wet with his hatred, back to a wrecked truck in a junk-yard where he might lie in the dark and dream that dream of his. "Bastits," Gurlick would mutter in the dark, hating . . . happy: "Lousy bastits."